THE SPIRIT OF LIBERTY MOON

TOUCHED
BY AN
ANGEL

THE SPIRIT OF LIBERTY MOON

Story and teleplay by MARTHA WILLIAMSON

MARTHA WILLIAMSON,
EXECUTIVE PRODUCER

Novelization by DAVIN SEAY

Based on the television series created by
JOHN MASIUS

THOMAS NELSON PUBLISHERS®
Nashville

Copyright © 1999 by CBS Broadcasting Inc.

Published in Nashville, Tennessee, by Thomas Nelson, Inc.

Scripture quotations are from the NEW KING JAMES VERSION of the Bible. Copyright © 1979, 1980, 1982, Thomas Nelson, Inc., Publishers.

Library of Congress Cataloging-in-Publication Data
Seay, Davin.
    The spirit of Liberty Moon / story and teleplay by Martha Williamson ; Martha Williamson, executive producer ; novelization by Davin Seay ; based on the television series by John Masius.
        p.   cm.—(Touched by an angel)
    ISBN 0-7852-7132-5 (pbk.)
    1. Williamson, Martha. II. Touched by an angel (Television program). III. Title. IV. Series.
PS3569.E237S55 1999
813'.54—dc21   99-22176
                                                                CIP

Printed in the United States of America
1 2 3 4 5 6 7 QPV 04 03 02 01 00 99

Prologue

The sky was a brilliant blue, as deep and clear as a dream of heaven, hung over the alpine meadows like the vault of a vast cathedral. In the lake below, a reflection could be seen in the sparkling water, a bright patch of purple with a long tail that fluttered even though no wind was ruffling the lake's surface.

Andrew ran across the meadow, trailing a line from a ball of string unraveling in his hands. Above him, the kite dipped and turned like a child at play, climbing ever higher, miraculously higher, into the brilliant sky where still no breeze had stirred. The string tugged between his fingers,

1

and he played out the line, letting the kite freely soar.

"Now you got it, Angel-Boy!" came a warm, throaty voice behind him, and he turned to see Tess, her salt-and-pepper hair catching the sun's rays and her broad smile beaming with a light all its own.

"But . . . ," said Andrew, out of breath from his fast dash across the meadow, "there's no wind, Tess . . ."

"Who said anything about wind?" Tess laughed, squinting up at the kite as it glided through graceful figure eights across the cloudless expanse. "It's a God thing!" Andrew shrugged and turned to follow Tess's gaze heavenward. A God thing . . . of course it was.

A short distance away, on the crest of a knoll overlooking the lake and the snowcapped mountains, Monica sat on a mossy rock that seemed to have been placed there for just that purpose. In her lap she cradled a sketch pad and from an artist's paint box at her side she dipped her brush into a bottle of jet-black ink.

Carefully, and yet with an assurance that comes

from experience, she layered the strokes of an ancient Chinese symbol across the thick, white paper. From broad to narrow, vertical to horizontal, the character began to take shape . . . the timeless balance of a timeless land.

As she worked, a white dove appeared, making its way across the sky, and Monica lifted her free hand without even looking up so the bird could land on her finger.

"It's my favorite word," Monica said as the cooing dove seemed to peer down at the paper. "Windowsill. Not much to look at in English, I'll admit, but in Chinese, why it's practically a work of art." She said the word again, the lilt of her brogue caressing the sound. "Windowsill."

"Windowsill?" Tess and Andrew stood beside her now, admiring her handiwork. Andrew held the kite, now a fragile, earthbound thing, as the bemused Tess shook her head. "Now when do you ever imagine you'll need to write down the word windowsill when we're in China?"

Monica put the finishing touch on her calligraphy and set down the brush, waiting as the warm sun dried the ink. It was so beautiful here.

So peaceful. If she had the choice she might linger in this meadow forever. But, of course, that wasn't up to her, and already she knew that they must be going soon.

"Did you know," she said, turning to her fellow angels beside her, "that the Great Wall of China is the only man-made structure you can see from the moon with the naked eye?"

"You mean you can't see all those squiggly lines?" asked Tess.

"What squiggly lines?" was Monica's reply.

"I think," Andrew added, "she means borders. International boundaries."

"Exactly," said Tess with a snort. "All those lines folks draw to keep themselves in . . . and to keep others out. That wasn't God's idea. No sir. See, the Father made some things that were never supposed to stay put. Like ideas. Important ideas." She pointed to the kite in Andrew's hands. "You take that little bit of cloth and sticks and string, for instance. An idea might not be much more than that. But you put a wind underneath it, and all of a sudden, that little notion is gonna take right off and fly. And it's gonna go where it needs to go, without bothering about somebody else's border. Because that's what it was made to do."

She turned to both of them with the loving yet challenging look a mother might share with her child as he takes his first step, or a captain with his crew on the verge of a new voyage. "That's what we're about to do . . . be the wind under somebody's wings. Of course," she added with a sigh, "whether they fly or not . . . well, that's up to them. All we can do is give them the chance."

Chapter One

The Manhattan morning was a busy blur of workaday rituals—a quick cup of scalding coffee, a mad rush for the uptown express, and a crush of commuters all hurrying to their offices and cubicles honeycombing the midtown skyscrapers, their deep shadows cast wide by the rising sun.

Perched serenely on the second-floor cornice of a gleaming office building, Tess, Monica, and Andrew surveyed the surging masses, watching intently for someone special, a face in the crowd set apart for a purpose. Monica looked up, past the skyline and the heavy, hanging traffic fumes to where a dove flew, straight and true . . . high above the hustle below.

Across the street from the plaza of the highrise, a bus lumbered to its stop, its passengers scattering in every direction. All, that is, except one.

Her name was Jean Chang, and as the angels on the ledge above caught sight of her, a quickening passed between them. Here she was. This was the one they had come for. And it was here, on a routine morning at an anonymous street corner in an uncaring city, that the story would begin to unfold.

Jean stood silently for a moment as pedestrians pushed around her. Her lustrous black hair, held loosely at her neck, caught the sun's muted rays, and her dark eyes, almond-shaped and earnest, watched as a security guard walked to the flagpole in the plaza and began hoisting the ropes to raise the Stars and Stripes. As Monica watched, she saw a flush of color pass over Jean's pale and perfect complexion. Something, the angel could see, was stirring in this beautiful, young Asian woman: an immigrant's pride, a reminder of hard-won freedoms, the blessings of liberty—renewed again at the sight of the waving flag.

"This isn't about flags or countries or politics," Tess explained, as if looking through a window into Monica's own thoughts. "This is about human hearts." Monica turned and smiled. She knew better than to be surprised or to question her supervisor's gifts and abilities. Their work had always been about trusting and believing that the Almighty would provide the guidance they needed as their situations required.

Like that silly, purple kite that Andrew had flown, now held carefully in Tess's hands, Monica knew it would do no good to ask why or what it was for. In time, plans and purposes would be revealed . . . even for a child's toy being carefully cradled by a wise angel.

On the street below, a series of events began to unfold with all the precision of a well-rehearsed play. Jean, suddenly stirred from her reverie, began to hurry across the street, worried now about being late for work. As she crossed the plaza, a sleek, black limousine pulled to the curb.

The driver jumped out and hurried around to the side, but before he could reach the door, his passenger had pushed it open and stepped out into the street, his ear glued to a cellular phone.

"I'm not interested in what they're doing over at Good Fun Toys," Edward Tanner snapped back at the voice on the line, then listened impatiently as he began to move across the plaza. He was tall, with dark hair, and a confident air set into his finely chiseled features.

Still perched forty stories high, Tess chuckled. "This is gonna be good."

Monica watched carefully as Edward began to move toward the lobby doors, looking past his expensive, tailor-made suit, with its French collar and glittering gold cuff links. She ignored his quick, no-nonsense tone of voice as he drove home his point over the phone. "Look," he continued, "we're only gonna consider this if it makes sense internationally." He listened before interrupting again. "—I know, I know. Alex is pushing China, but I'm leaning toward Mexico. No . . . I'm not making a move until I get all the facts . . ."

Beyond the clipped edge of his words, past all the trappings of conspicuous success, Monica thought she saw something. It was a flicker, a glow—faint but unmistakable—at the core of this handsome, and supremely self-assured young entrepreneur. "He's a good man," she said softly, trying to convince herself as much as Tess and Andrew. "There's a warm heart beating inside him. But it's hidden. Like a diamond in a pile of ashes." She turned to look at Tess again. "It's going to take some work to find it."

"There's a lot of work to be done here," replied Tess with an enigmatic smile as she pointed back down to the street. "Watch."

As Edward made a beeline for the lobby, Jean also crossed the plaza, heading toward the tall glass doors. For a moment it seemed as if the two might collide, but at the last moment, something happened that stopped Jean in her tracks. The soft breeze blowing through the concrete canyons stiffened, and the flag, loosely tied to its pole, began to flap and crack in the wind. As Jean and the angels watched, the rope went suddenly slack and the flag fluttered slowly to the ground, like a brightly colored handkerchief dropped by a passing giant.

Alarmed and without thinking, Jean hurried to the pole as the flag draped itself over the plaza's granite flagstones. She knelt to gather it up, directly in Edward's path, and it was only at the last moment that he looked up, narrowly avoiding stepping on her and the flag.

Monica caught her breath as Jean stood up with the flag in her arms, and for a quick moment looked into Edward's eyes. The noisy street seemed to grow quiet and, just then, she imagined that she could hear only the sound of two beating hearts. Edward slowly lowered the portable phone as Jean dropped her eyes and stepped to the side.

"Sorry," she and Edward said in unison, and they smiled, as people do when their eyes meet for the first time.

Then, as quickly as it happened, it was over. Edward nodded once and moved past Jean through the lobby doors. Jean began to raise the flag again, unaware that, behind her, Edward had turned to take one more look, lingering and slightly puzzled. She was a beautiful woman, no doubt about that. But what was the feeling that had passed between them? Had they met before? It was then that his phone rang again, the elevator door slid open, and life resumed, swallowing up the questions along with the answers.

Outside, Jean cinched the rope knot that held the flag in place. She looked up again, satisfied with her handiwork, and turned and headed toward the tall glass doors. Monica, Tess, and Andrew watched until she was out of sight and then sat for a moment in silence even as the street continued to empty of people and the new day began in earnest.

Tess sighed. "The courage of a single person can change history," she said at last as Monica and Andrew exchanged a look. She was giving them another clue, another hint of what was to come. And what was at stake. "But only if they answer the call when it comes."

"Will they answer the call?" asked Monica, gesturing to the doors behind which Jean and Edward had vanished.

"He may," was Tess's reply. "But he'll have only one chance."

"And what about her?" Monica's voice was barely above a whisper.

"For her," said Tess, "the chance will come a second time. And when it comes, she will know it." She looked to each of them and in her eyes was an expression at once hopeful and sad. "And that's why she may say no."

Across the plaza, a man pushed a hot dog cart and a homeless woman searched a garbage can for food. The angels perched in the morning sun were lost in their own thoughts. Monica looked up again into the sky, hoping for another glimpse of the dove. But above the towering building, all was an empty blue.

"And so it begins," she heard Andrew say.

Chapter Two

Tall windows framed the Manhattan skyline that was spread out like a panorama of prosperity. Edward Tanner moved purposefully across the lobby beneath a large sign, softly lit behind the reception desk and reading TANNER TOYS.

"Good morning, Mr. Tanner," chirped the trim and cheerful secretary behind the desk.

"'Morning, Janet," Edward responded with a preoccupation his employees had long since grown accustomed to. "Alex here?"

"Already in your office," answered Janet as she held out a sheaf of papers. "And these need your signature right away." It was too late. Edward had already disappeared down the hallway and through the double doors that sported his name embossed on a shiny, brass plaque.

Waiting for him inside was Alex Stella, the firm's high-strung attorney who at that moment was staring at a small purple object with a puzzled expression. What Alex lacked in height he made up for in nervous energy. He was looking at Tess's kite and the angel herself stood by, expectantly waiting to hear the lawyer's verdict.

"I don't know," Alex was saying in a puzzled tone. "You don't turn it on. It doesn't light up or shoot anybody. Kids are very sophisticated these days." He handed back the paper-stick-and-string construction. "I don't think it's our kind of toy."

"Oh, but that's where you're wrong," said the irrepressible Tess. "See, this toy isn't necessarily just for kids. It's portable. Why, it could fit right in your briefcase!"

Alex sighed. It was too early in the day to deal with crackpot toy inventors. "And why would I want a kite in my briefcase?" he asked.

"Well," answered Tess, pretending not to

notice his irritated tone, "you might want to fly it. You are a toy maker, after all."

"No," said Alex with exaggerated patience. "I'm a lawyer."

"Well then, Honey," Tess replied laughing, "you need to be flying a kite. And with this one, it doesn't matter where you are. It's guaranteed to soar as high as you want. Wind or no wind."

The remark perked Alex's interest. "You mean you've developed some sort of new technology or something?"

"See for yourself," said Tess, the twinkle in her eye unnoticed by the attorney. "Go ahead and check it out. Then give me a call. We'll talk."

From across the room, Edward cleared his throat, announcing his presence. Alex straightened immediately and, putting his hand on Tess's elbow, nudged her toward the door. "Fine," he said. "We'll be in touch." Tess let herself be moved along until they passed by Edward, where she suddenly stopped and looked the young executive straight in the eye. "You like kites, Mr. Tanner?" she asked.

"Sure," Edward answered. There was something about the intensity of this eccentric woman's gaze that stirred a strange feeling deep inside him. "Why not?"

"A kite's like a soul," Tess continued without breaking her gaze. "And you know, everybody likes to fly."

"This lady was just leaving," said Alex, as he pushed Tess to the door a little too forcefully, closing it behind her and leaning against it with a relieved sigh. "Toy inventors," he said shaking his head. "They're a whole different breed."

Edward was perusing the kite with casual interest. "A portable kite," he mused. "How does it work?"

"Never mind that," said Alex. "I got a call from Isaacson this morning. The investors are getting nervous. We've got to come up with a way to reduce costs. We just can't stall anymore. We've got to close the plants down south and get an operation started in China."

"I thought we were considering Mexico."

Alex shook his head again, in a gesture that mixed exasperation with affection. "How long have we known each other, Eddie?" he asked.

"I seem to remember a dorm room at Syracuse," said Edward with a smile.

"Exactly," said Alex. "And in all that time, have I ever steered you wrong?" He leaned across Edward's desk, picking up objects randomly—a paperweight, a fountain pen stand, a stapler—and turning them over. "Look at this: 'Made In China'; 'Made In China'; 'Made In China.' Look to the East, old friend. That's where the future is." Alex was getting excited now, waving his hands and moving in close to make his case. "I've got a file in my office this thick," he continued, holding his thumb and forefinger an inch apart. "Letters of introduction. Inquiries. Business proposals. All from Chinese companies. The labor's cheap. The raw material is bottom dollar. I'm telling you, Eddie, we've got people over there just begging to save us money."

Edward folded his arms and leaned back against his desk. The morning sun shone brightly through the penthouse window, and he thought to himself how much he valued his old college roomie. They'd been through so much together, building this company from scratch, and now it was all about to pay off as demand for Tanner toys made them the hottest newcomer in this fiercely competitive industry. Of course, if Alex said China was the place to be, he was probably right. His friend made a habit of doing his homework. But Edward only shook his head and looked doubtful. "But we don't know anything about China," he said, wanting to see the grand finale of Alex's performance.

"I'm way ahead of you," his friend replied with a grin. "I've already gotten a consultant. Expert on the whole Pacific Rim thing. She'll walk us through the import-export game—"

"Wait a minute," interrupted Edward. "She?"

Alex arched his eyebrows, his grin growing wider. "Thought that might pique your interest," he said. "Smart as a whip. And she's pretty, too."

Edward smiled ruefully. His friend knew him too well. "So," he said. "When do I meet this smart, pretty Pacific Rim expert?"

An intercom sounded on his desk and the voice of Janet announced: "Your nine o'clock is here."

"That'll be her now," said Alex, glancing at his wristwatch. "Right on time."

The door opened and Monica stepped into the room, dressed in a navy blue business suit, carrying a leather attaché case and looking, for all the world, like a successful young executive. A quick round of introductions and handshakes followed, during which the angel couldn't help but notice Edward's admiring gaze cast her way. The three sat down at the conference table, and Alex turned to Monica.

"So," he said. "My boss wants to know why we should build our new toy factory in China. Is that a question you can answer?"

"Indeed it is," replied Monica confidently and, snapping open her briefcase she pulled out a handful of papers and passed them around. "I've taken the liberty of preparing this prospectus based on your company's annual reports over the past five years and a comparative profit and loss statement based on current economic conditions on Mainland China. Of course, these figures must be adjusted for . . ." She faltered, then stopped as it became apparent that Edward Tanner was no longer paying attention to her words. He had, instead, picked up Tess's portable purple kite and was turning it over in his hands, like a small boy with a new toy.

"He's brilliant," said Alex, leaning over to whisper in her ear. "Quirky, but brilliant."

"Do you mind if we talk outside?" Edward asked suddenly and, without waiting for an answer, he rose and walked to the glass door that opened onto the penthouse patio. At once mystified and amused, Monica and Alex followed him into the bright sunshine high above the surging city.

A few minutes later, Edward was tugging at the kite string, while the tiny patch of bright purple was ducking and weaving, soaring over their heads and swooping between the looming shadows of the skyscrapers. It was a performance all the more amazing given the fact that, even at the dizzying height of the top floor, no wind was blowing.

"It's fascinating," Edward said, as much to himself as to the others, ". . . a physical impossibility."

"But a beautiful sight, nonetheless," Monica interjected, her head craned to follow the kite's random flight.

"Um, about our Chinese project—" Alex interrupted.

"Go for it" was Edward's quick reply, his eyes still fixed on the tiny dancing kite.

"Go for it?" echoed Monica, surprised by the snap decision.

Edward turned to her. "Alex thinks China is a good move. That's what I pay him for. Now, what am I going to pay you for?"

Monica turned to Alex, who beamed a broad grin and gave her the thumbs-up sign.

"Well," said Monica, "Mr. Stella has suggested that I accompany you to Beijing to evaluate the offers and help negotiate the trade agreements."

"Do you speak Chinese?" asked Edward, beginning to reel in the kite.

"A little," revealed Monica. "But I'd feel better if we had a competent translator."

"Anybody in mind?" As if by some magnetic force, the kite was pulled closer to Edward's outstretched hands.

Monica shrugged. "If I had a choice, I'd say someone in your company; someone who understands the toy business."

"There's that girl down in Contracts," Alex said and snapped his fingers as he tried to remember. "Jean something . . . She looks Chinese."

"Why don't you find out?" Edward said as the kite settled into his hand like a trained bird. He folded it up and passed it to his friend. "And while you're at it, try to figure out how this thing works."

Chapter Three

Alex looked across his desk to where Jean Chang sat stiffly in a straight back chair. The young lawyer, whose slight build and shock of sandy hair underscored his impulsive and boyish character, studied the beautiful, yet somber woman he had summoned to his office. Behind the attorney and slightly to one side, Monica stood, her arms folded, her face half hidden in the shadows of afternoon light. As she looked at Jean, she tried to penetrate the veil of sorrow that clung to her like a morning mist. What is it about her that makes me feel so sad? Monica thought to herself. What does she remember . . . and what is she trying to forget?

But it wasn't sadness flashing from Jean's dark eyes in that moment. It was anger and resentment, springing up like a hard shell around her.

"You ask me if I speak Chinese," she was saying with a cutting edge in her voice, "because I look Chinese?"

"Well, to tell you the truth—" Alex began, more than a little taken aback by her tone.

"I am not Chinese, Mr. Stella," Jean interrupted stiffly. "I am Korean. I was born in Seoul and raised in this country. So, even if I wished to accompany you to Beijing on your fact-finding trip, I would be of no use to you." She started to stand up. "May I go back to work now?"

"Please," said Alex, holding up his hands, "I just thought that—"

"—Because I look 'oriental,'" Jean shot back, "because my name is Chang, that I must be Chinese? Is that it?"

"None of us meant any disrespect, Ms. Chang," said Monica, stepping from the shadows and smiling gently.

"Sure," echoed Alex. "It really was an honest mistake."

"I understand," answered Jean, softly sighing. "But I have much work waiting for me."

"Of course," said Alex, standing up and escorting her to the door. "Thank you for coming in, Ms. Chang."

Her hand on the doorknob, Jean stopped and turned around. "I have worked for this company for three years," she said in a low voice. "And I have never been invited to this office. It has, at least, been enlightening."

Outside the door Jean stopped for a moment, leaning against the wall and waiting for the surge of emotions that had overcome her to subside. Her heart pounded in her throat, and she felt an unaccustomed rush of shame. What she had just done was wrong, against everything she believed and had ever been taught. But what choice did she have? How could she ever have made them understand?

These thoughts were still weighing heavily on her mind when Edward turned the corner and, catching sight of her, stopped in his tracks and smiled. Straightening herself and smoothing back her hair with a nervous gesture, Jean hurried down the hall, hoping he wouldn't notice the blush of color that had risen in her cheeks.

His smile turning quizzical, Edward pushed open the door to Alex's office.

"Was that the Chinese girl in Contracts you were talking about?" he asked his friend. "She looks promising."

"Forget it," answered Alex with a sigh. "She's Korean. Not Chinese. And not at all interested in a free trip to Beijing."

"So now what?"

Monica stepped forward. "I'm sure we can find a translator," she said with a comforting smile. "In the meantime, we should probably go over some of the proposals you've been getting." She paused before adding, "I have a favor to ask, though."

"What's that?" said Edward.

"It's lunchtime, and I'm starving," the angel said. "Can we do this over lunch? I know a nice little place not too far from here."

A quick cab ride across town deposited the

trio outside a small Chinese restaurant brightly decorated with paper lanterns and a gaudy New Year's dragon painted along one wall. Settling into a cozy booth and ordering a variety of savory house specials, Monica and the toy makers began going over the thick file of business proposals, interrupted from time to time by Alex's fumbling efforts to shovel food into his mouth with his chopsticks.

"Give it up, buddy," said Edward with a grin. "A fork is faster."

"No way," replied Alex as a morsel of Kung Pao chicken fell off the chopsticks and into his lap. "We're going to be doing a lot of this where we're going. I'd better get used to it now."

Monica, meanwhile, was busy prioritizing the pile of proposals, separating out a handful to one side of the table. "These four seem to be the most likely candidates for a joint venture," she explained.

"Will they understand that we're only going in as subcontractors?" asked Edward.

Monica nodded. "A lot has changed in China with the new open-door economic policy. No one is anxious to go back to the bad old days of state-run businesses. But they're having their own problems dealing with the consequences of a free economy. Crime. Corruption. That's one reason the government still has a heavy hand on the whole country."

"That's not really our problem," interjected Alex around a mouthful of fried rice. "We're interested in profits. Not politics." He glanced across to Edward. "Right, Boss? . . . Boss?"

But Edward wasn't listening, distracted this time by the familiar figure of a beautiful oriental woman coming down the street. "Isn't that the woman from Contracts?" he asked, pointing out the window.

The others, caught by the coincidence of seeing Jean again, stopped what they were doing and watched as she came closer. At a newsstand outside the restaurant she paused to pick up a paper, its headline printed in large, Chinese ideograms. Reading the front page, she pushed open the door and entered the eatery, unaware of the threesome watching her from the booth.

Alex and Monica traded a quick look as Jean stopped at the front counter to exchange a pleasant greeting with the wizened old woman at the cash register. Taking a nearby seat, she rattled off her order in Chinese to the waiter and then settled back to peruse the newspaper.

Edward leaned close over the table, asking in a low voice, "I thought you said she didn't speak Chinese. This is a Chinese restaurant, isn't it? And, unless I miss my guess, that's a Chinese newspaper she's reading."

Monica nodded. "Yes," she said. "That was a Mandarin dialect. I'm sure of it."

Alex was already halfway out of his seat. "I'm going to get to the bottom of this," he promised with grim determination. Striding up to Jean's table, he stood silently until, feeling his eyes on her, she looked up.

"Well, Ms. Chang," Alex said, summoning his most stern voice and pausing in an attempt to appear taller, "for a Korean you certainly seem to have a facility for ordering Chinese food in a Chinese restaurant in Chinese while reading a Chinese newspaper."

"Mr. Stella," Jean said, the color draining from her face.

"Ms. Chang—" he continued, cutting her off. "You are an employee of Tanner Toys, are you not?" Jean nodded, lowering her eyes as feelings of shame once again rushed over her.

Alex rolled on. "As an executive officer of Tanner Toys, I must ask you, since you have seen fit to lie about your background, what else you might be concealing from your employers."

Jean opened her mouth, but no words came out. From across the room she caught a glimpse of Monica and felt a momentary flash of gratitude at the empathetic look on the angel's face. She turned back to Alex, towering over her with arms crossed like an unforgiving taskmaster. She tried again to speak, hoping against hope that this time the words would come, when suddenly, with a bustle of bright color and unbridled energy, another familiar figure barged into the restaurant.

"Well, if this don't beat all!" exclaimed Tess, her voice lifting above the street noise that followed her in through the open door. Her self-confident happiness and ample personality seemed too big for the small space she occupied, and Monica smiled to herself as she watched her experienced friend take charge. "Imagine you and me getting a hankering for Chinese food at the exact same time, Mr. Stella."

Alex swallowed hard as he tried to maintain his dour demeanor. But it was clear he was no match for this force of nature called Tess. She grabbed him by the arm and began pulling him to a booth at the rear of the restaurant. "Pardon us," she said to Jean on the way past, "but Mr. Stella and I have some important business to discuss. Don't we, Mr. Stella?"

"I really don't have time—" Alex began, only to be stifled by Tess's full laugh. He was no match for this angel.

"Don't have time to hear my new marketing ideas for that itty-bitty kite?" she asked in disbelief. "Of course you do!" And with that, Tess pushed Alex into the corner booth, blocking his escape by sliding in next to him.

While Monica and Edward suppressed a giggle at Alex's dilemma, Monica cast a quick look to Jean from across the room, inviting her to join them. Jean hesitated for a moment before accepting, obviously still chagrined at being caught in a lie.

"I am so sorry," was the first thing she said as she sat down across from Monica and Edward. "I am afraid I have made Mr. Stella very angry."

"Don't mind him," said Edward, putting a comforting hand over hers. "He's a great lawyer, but he could use a little work in human relations."

Jean smiled gratefully, but the expression faded after a moment, washed away in the sense of vague sadness she carried around like an old and lingering memory. "I must confess that I did not tell you the truth today," she said, turning to Monica. "I am Chinese and, of course, I speak the language." She gestured to the old woman behind the counter. "But you could see that for yourself. I was born in Beijing and—"

"Please," Edward interrupted, his hand still covering hers. "You don't owe us an explanation."

"But I do!" cried Jean with sudden intensity and, in that moment, Monica knew that this young woman had been carrying around a heavy burden for far too long. It's almost, the angel thought to herself, as if she wants to tell us, to share her sorrow so that we might help carry its weight.

Jean took a deep breath, struggling to contain her emotions, even as her eyes glistened with tears. "I am a person of honor," she said in a low voice that trembled in spite of her best efforts. "At least I try to be. That is why I must tell you the whole truth. You see . . . if I were ever to go to Beijing again, I would not come back alive."

Chapter Four

The deep shadows of afternoon crept across the restaurant as the traffic outside slowed and the street seemed to empty in anticipation of the coming rush hour. The gold detailing of the painted dragon on the wall glinted softly in the wan light as the old Chinese woman at the counter dozed off, dreaming of another time in a faraway place.

In the booth in the back, Tess's voice could be heard chatting merrily away, while Alex nodded and sighed and tried desperately to get a word in edgewise. Tess seemed oblivious to his nervous discomfort, but in truth there was nothing that escaped the wise angel's attention. Of that Monica was sure when she glanced back and, for the space of a breath, caught Tess's attention and was rewarded with a wink. You go on, girl, Tess's look told her. I've got everything under control over here.

Monica turned back to Jean. "You wouldn't come back from Beijing alive?" she said. "That sounds a little dramatic, doesn't it?"

"Perhaps," replied Jean with a deep sigh. "It is part premonition, I admit. But it is also partly true. You see, as much as I dream of returning to my home, I know it is impossible now."

It was Edward's turn to look behind them, where Alex was getting an endless earful from Tess. "Well," he commented smiling, "it looks like we've got plenty of time to hear your story. That is . . . if you want to tell us."

Jean's eyes once again brimmed with tears, and Monica could see that something deep inside her was about to break. "It's all right," she said, the Irish lilt of her voice seeking to soothe the distraught young woman. "Everything you say will remain confidential. Just between us."

"Of course," murmured Edward. "Please don't be afraid."

Jean looked from one to the other, searching their eyes for a sign of their sincerity. At last she nodded, straightened up and, pushing aside her plate of uneaten food, asked in a calm and steady voice, "Have you ever heard of Tiananmen Square?"

"Of course," Edward answered at once. "I mean . . . as much as any American has."

Jean smiled, not quite dispelling the sadness behind her eyes. "Most Americans have only one image from that summer of 1989."

"The student." Monica nodded as she spoke. "Standing in front of the tank."

"Yes," Jean said. "He was very brave. But there were so many other students trying to make a change . . . make a difference . . . during those momentous days." She stared levelly across the table. "And I was one of them."

Monica turned to Edward, trying to gauge his reaction to Jean's revelation. He seemed interested, politely attentive, but unsuspecting that something unforgettable—tragic and deeply moving—was about to unfold.

From the kitchen came the distant sound of clattering dishes as the cooks began to prepare for the evening's patrons. A radio softly played Chinese pop music, and the fragrant smell of green tea wafted from the pot on the table. Jean closed her eyes, losing herself in the sounds and smells, so familiar yet so distant. These evocative reminders of her homeland carried her back, conjuring in cinematic detail the intimate scenes she had carried with her since childhood. She spoke in a voice so low it seemed to blend with the dull hum of the air conditioner, searching through her memory for the words to describe who she had once been and the terrible things that had happened to her as a small, innocent, and vulnerable child.

"I was a little girl in the sixties, during the Cultural Revolution," she began. "It was a terrible and cruel time in my country. Teachers, intellectuals, anyone suspected of being an 'enemy of the people' was in great danger. Many were arrested and sent to forced labor camps for 'reeducation.' Many more were tortured and murdered."

A shudder passed through her as she remembered those days, and vivid images moved over her mind like shock waves. It was all so clear— the day the young men in the green uniforms, waving the little red books over their heads, came to her home and dragged her father, kicking and screaming, out into the muddy streets. She could still see the hatred and contempt on their faces. It was as if it had happened yesterday . . . as if it were still happening, forever and ever in the echoing chambers of her memory.

"My parents were professors at the university," she said, forcing herself to continue, to keep talking, if only to hold the horrible images at bay. "One day the Red Guard came. They dragged my father into the streets and beat him as the whole neighborhood watched. They forced him to confess 'crimes' against the revolution."

Suddenly, in her mind, a shot rang out, loud and harsh. She started at the sound, but nothing could stop the flow of words now. Perhaps in telling her story, she could at last free herself from its tragic grip on her life. "My father was humiliated," she said, "and could not bear the shame. He shot himself, and his suicide was more than my mother could take. She became ill, but because of the shame my father had brought on our family, she did not receive proper medical care."

She remembered herself as a little girl, weeping at the deathbed of her mother; more men in uniform, coming to take her away, lifting her screaming into the back of a truck; a long, chilling ride deep into the countryside, and the iron gates of a grim and foreboding place.

"I was five years old when they took me to the orphanage," Jean continued. "It was cold and there was never enough to eat." She opened her eyes again, but the faraway look remained. "To this day I can never get used to having enough to eat."

Edward's polite disinterest had disappeared. Like Monica he was riveted to the flow of Jean's story. "What was the orphanage like?" he asked softly.

"A hard and lonely place," she replied. "I felt always . . . so alone."

As she spoke, it brought to mind one gray

afternoon, waiting for food at the end of a long line when her bowl was finally filled with the dregs of a thin soup, she made her way to a pallet bed, careful not to spill a drop of her precious meal until an older, stronger orphan stole it right out of her hands, sloshing some of the lukewarm liquid onto her soiled dress. But she didn't cry or make a single move. She was learning what it meant to suffer and how to endure.

"I thought that was the way the world was," Jean said now in a whisper. "Nothing belonged to you, not even your own thoughts. And you never dared to hope for something better."

Jean could recall being on the outskirts of the small village near the orphanage. In front of her a tableau was being acted out that her childish mind could not comprehend. A man, surrounded by more green-uniformed young people, was kneeling in the street, forced to wear a tall, conical hat and watch as books were hauled from his house and thrown onto a roaring bonfire.

"It was then that something caught my attention," Jean said, realizing for the first time that she had all along been describing to Monica and

Edward the pictures she saw unfolding before her mind's eye. "A single book lay in the street. Its pages were singed, but it had somehow escaped the fire. I reached down and snatched it up, hid it under my jacket and walked quickly away. It was a terribly dangerous thing to do," Jean said. "But even as a little girl, I knew I had nothing left to lose." From across the table, her stare pierced the hearts of her listeners as she said with utter conviction, "And what I found in that book would change my life forever."

"What was it?" asked Monica breathlessly.

"I couldn't read the words," Jean admitted shyly, "but there was a picture in the front of the book of a beautiful lady. She held her head proudly. She seemed to be afraid of nothing. I wanted so much to be like her."

She remembered running to a far corner of the orphanage yard, where there was a pile of rocks. Carefully moving one of the stones aside, she hid the book away, deep in a crevice where no one would ever find it.

"It was the only thing that was mine," she continued. "And I sometimes think it was the only thing that kept me alive over all the years that followed."

The pictures in her memory were growing dim now, as seasons swirled by like autumn leaves before a winter wind. Vague impressions moved across her vision, images of a young girl blending into images of a young woman, a process of years compressed into a few fleeting moments. But when she could clearly remember what happened next, it was that same pile of rocks at the far end of the barren dirt playground that rose up before her. Jean reached down to move away the stone of the secret hiding place, taking out the precious book yet one more time.

But the hand that held the book was older, the face wiser, with the first traces of the sadness that Jean would carry with her into adulthood. She was a teenager now, still an orphan but ready, at last, to step out into the world and make her own way.

"Ten years later Mao was dead," she continued, pausing only to take a sip of tepid green tea, as if it were an elixir that would bring her

memories into sharper focus. "China was chang-
ing. People began again to live, to stop looking
always over their shoulders and waiting for the
soldiers to pound at the front door. As soon as
I was able, I left the orphanage and made my
way to Beijing. The only things I took with me
were a few clothes and my precious book. I was
determined to learn to read its words, to discover for myself who the proud lady in the picture really was."

The images in Jean's mind began to melt
together, a swirl of scenes and moments that
seemed to rise from her memory by themselves.
A classroom crowded with college students copy-
ing their lesson off a blackboard; then a group
of happy, laughing young people crowded into
a campus café, loudly trading jokes and opinions.
Among them was Jean, flanked by two young
men, all enjoying one another's company. In her
mind, Jean could see clearly the young man who
carried her books. He was hardly more than a
boy really, yet his smiling face was lit with love
as he gazed at her. She heard a voice, her own,
and realized once again that she was still talking,

describing for Monica and Edward what was rising from her memory.

"I went to school to study English," she was telling them. "It was there that I met my husband. Gus and I, and his best friend, George, became inseparable, united by our love of all things Western—art, music, literature . . ."

"Your husband's name was Gus?" asked Monica, hardly daring to interrupt the flow of Jean's reminiscences.

Jean smiled, and in that moment, the melancholy that clouded her eyes seemed to lift. "We gave each other nicknames, as young people do. Our friend Wei Guo called himself George, after George Washington. We called my husband Gus after his favorite sculptor, Auguste Rodin . . . you know, the one who carved *The Thinker*." She stopped for a moment to assume the pose of the famous statue, furrowing her brow, putting her hand to her chin and trying to look very serious. Edward laughed. The charm and simple grace of the young woman was beginning to captivate him.

"After so many years of being cut off from the

rest of the world," Jean continued, picking up the thread of her narrative, "the people were hungry for information, Suddenly, there were books, magazines, newspapers, everywhere."

Jean's words brought back to her vivid images of her past, images of walking through a crowded marketplace, past a street vendor selling old and dog-eared books laid out on a dingy sheet spread on the ground. She stopped and stooped down, with the awkward movements of a woman in the last months of pregnancy, holding her swollen belly with one hand as she picked up a book that had caught her attention. Paying the vendor for her purchase, Jean leafed through the volume as she walked away, pushing her pigtails behind her shoulders when they fell across the pages. She flipped past a full-page photograph, stopped and turned back, her eyes growing wide with wonder. There she was again: the proud lady, her gaze fixed to the future, a book of justice cradled in one hand, a torch of freedom burning in the other.

Stopping in the middle of the crowded marketplace, Jean reached into her bag and pulled out a small package, lovingly wrapped in an old cloth. She opened it, revealing the most precious possession of her lost and lonely childhood—the tattered and half-burned book she had rescued from the flames all those many years ago. Turning to the page she knew so well, she compared the picture there with the one from her new book. They were the same. But in this book was a caption. The Statue of Liberty, she read, as her eyes filled with tears, and she moved down the street, rejoicing, knowing at last the name of the lady who had given her inspiration and guidance for so long.

Jean wiped the tears that welled up in her eyes now as she sat in a big-city café, thousands of miles and a lifetime from those days she was remembering. But there was no time to cry over what had been . . . and what could never be. She had to continue with her story, a story she had kept inside for far too long.

"With the population growing so quickly," she said, wiping her eyes dry, "the people were instructed that, for the good of the state, we should only have one child. Everyone, of course, wanted a boy, because, in my country, a boy brings honor. But that day I bought the book and knew at last the name of the proud lady, I realized that the Statue of Liberty, a symbol of freedom for so many oppressed people around the world, was not a man . . . but a woman." Her voice grew thin and faint and she struggled to suppress a sob. "I knew that if there was a place in this world for a woman to become a beacon of freedom, then there would always be hope for me . . . and for my daughter."

"You had a little girl," Monica said, smiling at the thought of a tiny infant in Jean's loving arms.

Jean nodded, and now there was no stopping the tears from flowing down her cheeks. "I named her Piao Yue. It means 'Free Moon,' but in English the meaning is closer to 'Liberty Moon.'"

"Where is she now?" asked Edward, and from the stricken expression that crossed Jean's face, he was immediately sorry he had asked.

"I . . . don't know," was all she managed to say before standing up. "Will you excuse me?"

she asked before moving quickly to the back of the restaurant and through the door of the ladies' room.

Chapter Five

$\mathcal{E}$dward sat back in the booth, exhaling deeply as if remembering to breathe for the first time since Jean had begun her compelling story. He cast a quick look at Monica, and the two shared a moment of silent agreement: This young woman, as fragile as a porcelain Chinese vase, had survived so much with such strength and dignity.

From across the room Edward noticed that Alex was still cornered by Tess, who chattered happily on with no signs of slowing down. He had forgotten all about his friend, a fact that Alex seemed painfully aware of as he implored Edward with a desperate look to rescue him. Edward smiled, gestured him over, and with palpable relief Alex tore himself away.

"Do me a favor," he said in an urgent whisper as he arrived at the table and leaned over to Edward. "Check your watch and shake your head."

Trying his best to look stern and serious, Edward obliged. "Good," said the frazzled lawyer. "Now frown some more and shrug like there's nothing you can do about it."

Once again, Edward granted the request as Monica hid her own laugh behind her hand. Alex, with his alibi in place, turned to Tess at the far booth and shrugged, even as he grabbed his coat and began scuttling toward the front door. "Darn!" he called out to the angel across the room. "Wish I could stay but we've got a conference call with Hong Kong back at the office that we've simply got to take." He turned to Edward. "So . . . hadn't we better be going, Boss?"

"You go," Edward said, no longer able to hide his amusement. "I'm going to stick around for a while."

"Okay," replied the surprised Alex, not at all

sure he understood what was going on, but only too glad to escape from Tess. He glanced over his shoulder and, seeing that the angel had gotten up herself and was moving toward them, rushed out the front door.

"So, Mr. Tanner," Tess said as she arrived at the table. "You tried out my kite yet?"

Edward nodded. "It's quite amazing," he admitted. "I'm planning a trip to China, actually, and I'd like to take it with me to see what they think of it."

"Oh," said Tess with a hearty laugh as she gathered her coat and purse. "They're gonna love it. You wait and see." And, with a wave of her hand and a flash of color and motion, she disappeared out the door.

As they watched her go, Edward turned with a half-apologetic shrug to Monica. "You get a lot of crazy inventors in the toy business," he explained.

Monica nodded, then, after a moment, asked, "You seem like such a serious fellow, Mr. Tanner. What are you doing making toys, anyway?"

Edward looked at her, slightly taken aback by her bold question. But there was something in the angel's eyes, something that reassured him that, with this woman, it would be safe to let down his guard. "Maybe I'm just having the childhood I never got." The words sounded unintentionally sad and self-pitying, even as he said them. He straightened a little, shaking off the introspective mood. "But it's more likely about making money. See, parents will always spend more on their kids than they do on themselves."

"I think parents everywhere are like that," Monica agreed, then asked in the same gently probing tone, "Do you have children?"

"No," was Edward's abrupt reply. "Never married."

"But why?"

Edward shrugged again. "Never found the right one, I guess."

As if on cue, Jean suddenly returned, her eyes dry now, her composure regained. "It's late," she said. "I must be getting back to work." She reached for the bill the waiter had brought for her meal, but Edward was faster. For a moment their hands touched, a moment made longer as Edward kept his finger resting lightly on Jean's delicate wrist. A look passed between them, the brief spark of some special connection that, as Monica watched, she could not help but notice with a soft, inward smile. "Let me, please," Edward said as Jean's eyes dropped modestly from his gaze. He swept up both bills and absentmindedly grabbed the fortune cookies on the tray and slipped them into his jacket pocket.

A few moments later, the three were heading back across town in the back of a taxi. The streets were starting to fill again as the afternoon wound down and people hurried to finish up the business of the day. Edward stared out the window, lost in thought, while Jean looked straight ahead, intent only on maintaining the fragile equilibrium she had achieved after so many unsettling memories. Monica knew instinctively that it was up to her to continue what had begun, seemingly by accident, at this momentous lunch.

"Tell us more about your husband," she said as casually as she could.

"I think I have bored you enough with my story," Jean answered.

"No, please," interjected Edward, turning

from the window. "We want to hear." He looked her straight in the eye. "I want to hear."

Jean smiled, grateful for the kindness of these strangers. She found herself anxious now to complete her story and, with it, a cleansing and healing to the wounds she had carried for so long.

"Gus was the one who taught me that only through democratic principles could China be truly free," she explained. "He and George and I began to publish articles and pamphlets calling for political reform. But it was very risky. Many activists already had been arrested, sentenced to prison, and punished severely for criticizing the government. But we believed . . . we believed so strongly that it was our time to stand up and speak out, to become the voice of our people, a people who longed for a better life."

Now, along with the images, came smells and sounds and sensations that sharpened the memories evoked by Jean's words: the sharp odor of printer's ink; the bleary-eyed exhaustion of long nights under bare electric bulbs as the mimeograph machine churned out pages with a mesmerizing rhythm; the sounds of a small child, her precious Liberty Moon, playing happily at her feet with the discarded papers that fell from the table where she was busy binding and stapling their political broadsides.

"It was a very exciting time," Jean said as the taxi turned onto a congested street and bleating horns clamored around them. "A time of great change."

Jean's recollections were as clear and fresh as a memory of yesterday, even though they had happened so many years before. It was as if the emotion attached to each of the pictures from her past brought it that much more sharply into focus. Surging crowds of protesting students; mass marches through the ancient streets of Beijing; the weakened bodies of hunger strikers being cared for by eager, idealistic young people with brightly colored swatches of cloth wrapped around their heads. And the enormous expanse of Tiananmen Square, seething with a restless horde of humanity, gathered together to lay claim to their inalienable rights.

"We were only students, leading peaceful protests," Jean said, her voice low against the dull groan of idling car engines around them. "We asked only that leaders listen to our ideas for reform, and to our amazement, ordinary citizens from every walk of life joined our movement. Our marches got larger and larger as people grew excited and hopeful for the first time in years. All across my homeland, demonstrations erupted, and my group of twenty-year-old students who had started it all suddenly found ourselves at the front of a national movement, challenging the most powerful men of our nation."

She vividly recalled every dramatic moment from those days: her protesting classmates, men and women lying on the cobbled expanse of Tiananmen Square, cheered in their self-imposed acts of starvation by farmers and peasants and factory workers; the voices of government officials loud and blaring through bullhorns, demanding that the freedom marchers disperse. It was strange to think that so many of her memories had been shared with the whole world, as televisions flashed pictures of the Square around the globe. One thing was certain—the feeling of an unfettered passion for freedom was as strong just then in the back of the cab as it had been in those heady days outside the gates of the Forbidden City.

"The government was infuriated," Monica recalled. "It must have been a frightening time."

"Yes." Jean nodded. "Saving face is very important to the Chinese. We had embarrassed our leaders in front of the whole world. They considered us traitors, and we knew they would never forgive what we had done. Some of us could not face the wrath of our elders and turned away. Our friend George, for example—he never took part in the demonstrations on the square. Instead, he stayed home and watched over little Piao Yue. It was all he could do to help the cause, and no one blamed him. We all did what we could and, together, it was almost enough."

"And your husband?" Edward asked. "What did he do?"

"He joined the hunger strikers," Jean explained. "I brought him water every day and tried to keep him comfortable. All around us in the square, the crowds grew larger day by day. Everyone who was there in those last few hours remembers it differently. But none of us will forget the night they erected 'The Goddess of Democracy.' We had occupied the square for seventeen days, and the government had declared martial law. We knew our time was running out, and morale was very low. It was then that the students from the art college surprised us with our very own statue of liberty. She could be seen all across Tiananmen, like a beacon for our cause."

"Tiananmen," Edward wondered out loud. "What does that mean?"

Jean turned to look at him and, for the first time, her eyes flashed with bitterness and anger. "The Gate of Heavenly Peace," she said, the irony dripping from her voice. "But there was no peace in that place. The army and our leaders made sure of that."

Chapter Six

The square, for those few weeks, had captured the attention of the whole world. And there, among the crush of humanity, was the small, round face of Jean's daughter, Piao Yue, staring up in rapt fascination at the towering figure of democracy's goddess, her figure a rough approximation of the Statue of Liberty that had sparked Jean's hopes and dreams so many years before.

"You took your little girl to the square?" Jean heard Monica ask.

"Of course," she replied. "You must understand how we felt. This was an historic time for my country and my people. I wanted Liberty Moon to always be able to say that she had been there as a witness when democracy was born in China."

Jean experienced once again the almost-overwhelming feelings of being separated for so long from her only child and the emotion brought with it another vividly remembered incident from those momentous days. While the protesters huddled in their rough shelters and homemade tents, the little girl sat on the pavement, drawing a design with the charcoal from a burnt twig pulled from one of the cooking fires. The sketch was simple yet drawn with sure strokes by the child—the unmistakable shape of a half-moon, with a simple flame burning at its crescent. Piao Yue looked up with wide eyes at her mother, seeking approval for her handiwork, and Jean smiled as she slowly pronounced two words in English. Her daughter followed suit, comically wrapping her mouth around the unfamiliar syllables that made up her name . . . "Liberty . . . Moon."

"I remember in those days thinking much about the moon that shone over our heads at night," Jean continued as the taxi crawled through the crosstown snarl. "I wanted to show my little girl what her name meant in English, and I would point to the moon in the sky. I told my daughter that no matter where she was," Jean continued, "if she ever felt lost or alone . . . if she ever needed me, all she had to do was look up at the moon and know that somewhere, I was looking at the same moon, too. But for the word liberty, all I could do was describe for her the picture I had seen in the book, the statue with the flame of freedom held so high."

Even as the memory flooded over her, filling her eyes once more with tears, Jean could almost hear the small, piping voice slowly speaking out the strange words in English. "The Statue . . . of . . . Liberty." A loud car horn outside the window brought her back to the moment, and she quickly wiped her eyes, straightening her shoulders. She must be brave, she must be strong. For so long it was all she had known . . . the only way to hang on.

She turned again to the passengers who not only shared the backseat of the taxi, but her own journey through the years. Monica smiled—a comforting sign of empathy and encouragement. "Jean," she said softly. "You don't have to continue if you don't want to. We would understand if—"

"No," Jean interrupted. "I want you to know . . . everything." She blinked rapidly almost as if reacting to the glare of photographic flash-bulbs at the Square. She recalled the fleeting glimpse of a government official taking incriminating pictures of Jean as she read aloud from one of the pamphlets printed in their kitchen. It was at that moment that she understood the awful truth: There was no going back now. The events at the Gate of Heavenly Peace would change everything in their lives . . . forever.

"The military moved in and surrounded us," she continued in a voice almost too low to hear. "It was only a matter of hours before the crack-down would come." A dazed look passed over her eyes as she tried to bring order to the rush of recollections. "None of us ever really believed that they would use real bullets that day. But even then, my husband Gus refused to leave.

He wanted to continue his hunger strike to the end. I had no choice. I had to leave him and take Piao Yue home, out of danger. I left her with George and ran back to the square as quickly as I could."

Her breath quickened as the pace of the story increased. It was as if she were suddenly there again, frantically pushing against the crush of people, some moving toward the square, others rushing away as tanks and armored personnel carriers moved into position. Her face was pale in the afternoon light leaking through the taxi's dirty window, and her eyelids fluttered as she closed them against the chaos and fear that the memories brought rushing back.

"The soldiers received their orders and began moving toward the demonstrators in tanks and trucks," she said, her voice breathless now as the words tumbled out. She could hear gunshots, mingled with the screams of people and the stench of something burning. "They killed many, many people in the city that night, and the killing continued over the next few days."

"And Gus?" asked Edward, now totally caught

up in the suspense of Jean's harrowing account. "What happened to Gus?"

"I don't know," said Jean, turning to him with a look of sorrow and resignation that caused his heart to lurch in his chest. "But I heard later that he had been shot in the back."

How could one person endure so much? Edward found himself thinking. What kept her going? It was a thought that dispelled any feelings of pity he had been feeling, replaced now with pure admiration for the spirit of survival embodied in this small and seemingly frail woman.

"When I couldn't find him at the square, I looked for him in the local hospital," Jean was saying, "but everywhere was chaos and confusion. Within hours of the first attack, they were arresting everyone we had known. I knew that I was in danger as well, so I rushed back home to find George and my daughter. But—" she choked now, fighting a losing battle against her tears and the sorrow she had held back for so long. "But they were gone. In one day I had lost my husband, our best friend . . . and my daughter."

But Jean's ordeal had been far from over. As

the taxi finally broke free of the congested street and began a quick dash down a side street toward the office tower of Tanner Toys, Jean, too, seemed to be racing against some fearsome pursuer, chasing her down through the years, hunting her with merciless resolve and driving her into a trap from which there was no escape.

Jean remembered rushing from the Beijing apartment, calling out to George and Liberty Moon. There, in the street, she stopped cold as she saw a green-clad soldier interrogating one of her neighbors down the block. The man caught sight of her and, chattering excitedly, pointed her out, even as she dashed back into the block of buildings with the soldier in hot pursuit.

Now her memories began to grow dark, stuffy, and claustrophobic. Fear filled her nostrils, cutting off air in a confined space, as through the narrow crack in a door she saw and heard the soldiers ransacking her home. She saw their jackbooted feet move by her as dishes crashed and furniture was shattered, and she squeezed her knees tightly beneath her chin, trying to fold herself into an ever-smaller bundle.

"You hid in a kitchen cupboard?" Edward asked her, his voice undercut with shock and frank admiration. "For how long?"

"I'm not sure," said Jean as the cab pulled up to the plaza outside the building where she had arrived for work this same eventful day, which now seemed a thousand years long. "It must have been several nights. At last, I found the courage to leave. I found people in the neighborhood . . . friends who were willing to help me, and I was able to escape to Hong Kong. From there, I made my way to America and got my green card. I actually did finish my studies at Berkeley, as I told Mr. Stella. That much was true. And now, I have made America, the land of Lady Liberty, my home. There is nothing left for me in China."

The cabdriver turned from the front seat, ready to collect his fare. Edward ignored him. "And George," he asked. "Did you ever hear from him again?"

Jean shook her head. "I tried to find him, using my old connections in Beijing. But it was no use. He probably changed his name and started a new life. I am afraid that if I keep trying I will jeopardize his safety."

"And Liberty Moon?" Monica asked, almost afraid to hear the answer.

But before Jean could respond, the taxi driver cut in with an impatient, "Hey, buddy, I don't got all day here. You owe me six bucks."

With an exasperated sigh, Edward reached into his pocket, pulling out a handful of bills and the fortune cookies he'd taken from the table at lunch.

"Chinese people are good people," Jean said in answer to Monica's question. "They love children. George has taken care of my daughter. I am sure of it." But the tone of her voice was anything but sure, and the deep sadness that lingered there seemed to permeate the confines of the cab, silencing even the surly driver.

It was then that Jean smiled, trying with gracious charm to lighten the mood she had created with her story. "No one wants their fortune cookie?" she asked, pointing to the little wrapped packets in Edward's hands. "You know, we don't have such cookies in China."

Edward smiled. "I guess it's only in America that you have the freedom to crack open your own future. And I already know what mine says: 'Go home and count your blessings.'" He stopped for a moment as the import of his words sunk in. "I'm sorry," he hastened to add. "That didn't come out the way I meant."

"No," Jean reassured him. "I understand what you mean. I, too, have many blessings, Mr. Tanner. I am alive. I am free." She smiled, and the expression touched something deep in the business executive, in a place too long neglected. "And I always have the moon to look at." She opened the cab door. "Good-bye, and thank you for listening."

"No," said Edward. "Thank you. For sharing." He reached out and took her hand, shaking it for a moment longer than decorum called for and letting go only when he saw the expression on Jean's face, a look of surprise at the emotional connection conveyed in his simple touch.

Monica and Edward watched as Jean crossed the plaza and disappeared through the lobby doors. As they, in turn, emerged into the waning light of afternoon, the angel faced him and asked, "Have you gone over these business proposals with Alex?"

"No," said Edward, still staring at the place where Jean had just been. "Why?"

"There's something I think you should see," was all that Monica would say.

She pulled a piece of paper from the file proposals, and handed it to Edward. It was a business letter, proposing a management partnership between Tanner Toys and a Chinese company. But it wasn't the content of the letter that caught and held Edward's attention: it was the logo at the top of the page. A half-moon with a simple flame burning at its crescent hung suspended over the words Liberty Moon International Management.

Chapter Seven

The paper lay on Edward's desk amid a jumble of memos, manuscripts, and the various untested trinkets and gizmos that were a toy maker's stock-in-trade. Outside, beyond the double doors of his office, the hustle and bustle of his successful business went on unhindered, the relentless wheels of commerce turning out its required percentage of the gross national product.

But here, in the well-cushioned silence of the executive suite, it felt as if time stood still. Edward, behind his desk, looked up at Monica, perched on the desk edge with a look that gave him an unfamiliar and not entirely welcome feeling that something was now required of him. Something extraordinary.

"So," he said testily, "what do you want me to do?"

"This has been put into your hands for a reason," Monica replied.

Edward sighed and looked down at the paper in front of him again, hoping against hope that what he had seen there wasn't what he thought it was.

"What reason might that be?" he snapped back, looking up from the proposal and back to Monica. "So I can tell Jean there's a Chinese company called Liberty Moon, and she can wonder about it for the rest of her life?"

"No," Monica said, her voice still calm, but beneath it, a steely determination. "So she can do something about it."

"She can't go back to China, if that's what you mean," Edward shot back.

"No," admitted Monica. "Not without help she can't."

Edward threw up his hands. "No. No way. I'm not getting involved in this."

Monica leaned over the desk, the better to drive home her point. "She's got a better chance of getting into Beijing if she's with a group of American businesspeople," the angel insisted.

Edward shook his head emphatically. "Forget it. I can't take the risk. Besides, what can one man do about it anyway? It's history."

"He can stand up, the way Jean stood up."

"Look," Edward said exasperated. "I'm just a businessman."

"And Jean was just a student," Monica insisted tenaciously. "Think about the courage on that woman's face. I know you saw it. Now ask yourself—'Would I have the same courage to stand up when it really counts?' This is your chance to answer that question . . . your chance to make a difference."

"A difference?" Edward spat. "You don't get it, do you? I just want to make a profit."

Monica shook her head, forming the words carefully, aiming for maximum impact. "'What does it profit a man,' Edward, 'if he gains the whole world but loses his soul?'"

"Don't talk to me about souls," the executive shot back. "I gave that up a long time ago."

"I don't believe that," the angel replied. "You've locked it up somewhere, like you've locked up that purple kite in your briefcase. You might take it out to analyze it, see what makes it tick, but you're afraid to really let it go, to watch it soar. But soaring is what souls are made to do, Edward."

"Ever heard of a crash landing?" he asked, looking up at her with a cynical glance.

"Yes, of course," Monica said. She could sense something stirring in this mortal man and could almost hear the questions he found himself suddenly asking in the silent place of his heart, maybe for the first time. "It's true. The higher you dare to go, the farther you may fall. But isn't that better than never having flown at all?"

Her words seemed at last to reach a place that Edward could not protect with the armor of his disdain. He stood and walked to the window, looking out across the vast expanse of steel and concrete. Monica came up behind him and took in the vista as well, so different from the fresh and unsullied alpine meadow where this journey had begun. She peered though the window high into the fading afternoon light. "Have you ever noticed," she said, as Edward became aware of the angel at his shoulder, "how even on the sunniest days, you can sometimes still see the moon?"

He turned to her, shaking his head in disbelief, hardly willing to admit to himself what he was about to do. "Don't tell Alex," he said. "He'd blow a gasket. And if this turns into an international incident, you better believe I'm going to deny everything. I never knew her. I never knew you. I never knew anyone."

Monica couldn't help but smile. "'The secretary will disavow any knowledge of your actions.' Sounds very mysterious, Mr. Tanner. Or should I say, 'Mr. Bond'?"

Edward only had time to shoot her a wry look before moving back to his desk, flicking the intercom switch, and asking his secretary to summon Jean Chang up from the Contracts Department, a floor beneath them. While they waited for her to arrive, Monica watched the young executive carefully and, by the time a knock was heard on the office door, she was convinced that the nervousness she saw on his face had less to do with provoking an international incident than the anticipation of seeing this lovely young woman again. Human beings, she thought to herself with a secret grin, are so predictable sometimes.

Jean entered with a shy smile. "I didn't expect to see you both again so soon," she said.

"Jean," said Edward, the seriousness of his tone wiping the smile from her face. "There's something I want to show you . . . something Monica found in the file of business prospects from China." Handing over the proposal, he watched her face as she scanned it, and saw the blood drain from her flawless, porcelain skin at the sight of the Liberty Moon logo. "Please. Sit down," he said, the concern showing in his voice. "Can I get you something to drink?"

Jean just shook her head, still stunned at the paper she held in her hands and the implications it held for her future.

"It's a consulting firm in Beijing," Monica explained. "They help American companies open manufacturing plants and manage them."

"Of course," Edward was quick to add, "there's nothing to indicate that the man who runs it is your friend George."

"Except the company name and the logo design," Monica countered significantly.

Jean studied the letter. "It is signed Wu Wa Guo," she pointed out. "George's name was Wu Wei Guo. That's very similar. He could have changed his name"—she continued, looking from Edward to Monica with a slight smile on her lips—"George never did like his name."

"Well," said Edward, hoping against hope that the situation might somehow take a different turn, "it's a long shot—" A look from Monica caught his eye, an expression mixing reproof with a gentle pleading. Please, she seemed to be saying with her eyes, give this a chance. Edward sighed, then cleared his throat. "But if you think it's worth looking into—"

Jean looked up to him, her eyes glistening in the deep shadows of the approaching twilight.

"To see my daughter again, Mr. Tanner," she whispered, "is worth my life."

Chapter Eight

The jumbo jet arched high over the glittering lights of the Manhattan nightscape, its engines roaring across the ink black sky, making a slow turn around the teeming metropolis before heading north for its long journey over the roof of the world to the far side of the planet.

Inside the pressurized, climate-controlled, and softly lit confines of the first class cabin, Monica and Jean sat together as beneath them the earth fell away and a crescent moon appeared in the window, like a beacon guiding them home. A stewardess walked serenely through the cabin, handing out newspapers and magazines, an offer

Jean, pale and thin-lipped, refused when the cart passed by them.

"Try to relax," Monica said, laying her hand on Jean's arm. "Everything's going to be fine."

"No," said Jean, turning to her with a look that seemed to contain a lifetime of uncertainty. "This isn't going to work."

"Of course it will," replied Monica reassuringly. "And even if it doesn't, what's the worst that can happen? They'll stop you at customs, see that your passport is expired, and send you back."

The doubt in Jean's eyes was not dispelled. "How strange," she said, half to herself, "to have to try to sneak back into your own country."

The pilot's voice crackled over the intercom. "Ladies and gentlemen," he said with a friendly Midwestern twang, "our estimated flying time to Beijing this evening is twenty-two hours and eighteen minutes. We'll be cruising at an altitude of thirty-five thousand feet, and once we've reached it, I'll turn off the seat belt sign and you'll be able to move freely about the cabin. In the meantime, those of you on the left side of the plane might want to take a look out the window as we pass the Statue of Liberty."

The announcement lit up a wide smile on Jean's face as she turned to peer out the window, cupping her eyes to block out the overhead lights. Monica smiled. It's a good sign, she thought to herself, a hopeful sign.

Across the aisle, Edward and Alex huddled, already poring over the business offers that would be awaiting their decision almost immediately upon arrival. The lawyer had spread out the file of proposals on both their folding trays and, though Edward tried to appear interested, he found his eyes drifting across the cabin to where Jean sat.

"I think we can narrow it down to these three prospects," Alex was saying, tapping a pile of papers he had set to one side. "But I'm still not sold on this Liberty Moon outfit." He snagged a passing stewardess. "Can we get some coffee here?" he said tersely.

Edward smiled, adding "Please" and indicating two cups. It was going to be a long flight. "Liberty Moon might be a little small for our purposes," he admitted to his associate. "But that could mean more personal attention. We're going to be in business with these people for a long time." He paused, trying to find a way to phrase his next question until deciding it was best to just come out with it. "Alex?" he asked. "What's your take on human rights?"

"I believe everybody's got a right to be human," the lawyer quipped with a smirk.

"I'm serious," Edward insisted. "Some people claim we're too soft on the human rights issue because corporate America wants a piece of the China pie. They say we lack . . . courage."

"I couldn't agree more," Alex said, still unsure of what his boss's point might be. "We're lacking courage all the way to the bank. One point two billion people, and they've all got kids. And all those kids are going to want their very own Tanner toy." He looked around. "Didn't we order coffee? I thought this was first class . . ."

"Of course," Edward continued, thinking out loud, "we can use our trade influence to bring about political reform."

Alex, now genuinely puzzled, turned to stare

at Edward. "Since when did you start getting interested in your fellowman?" A long moment passed before the light of understanding went on in his eyes. "Oh," he said, "I get it. It's your fellow woman that's got your interest." He leaned forward for a confidential whisper. "Look," he confided, "forget it. She's one cold fish."

But Edward was paying no attention, once again drawn to the pale and delicate face of Jean as she turned from the window, a light still burning in her eyes from the sight of Lady Liberty out the airplane window.

Hours later, only Alex's overhead light was still turned on as he continued to crunch numbers and sort options for the upcoming meetings. Beside him, Edward had thrown a blanket over himself to catch a quick nap and, across the aisle, Jean's sleeping head had dropped onto Monica's shoulder. As the jet passed over the frozen wilderness of the North Pole below them, Monica woke from her own light sleep, sensing a familiar presence in the first-class cabin. Careful not to wake her sleeping companion, she peered down the rows of seats.

There he was. Andrew, the gentlemanly Angel of Death, had joined them on their journey. Monica nodded in recognition and sat back in her seat with a sigh. Whatever might happen on the far side of their destination would try the courage of them all. Of that much she was sure.

The dawn broke dirty and smudged over the endless outskirts of the Imperial City as the plane began its final descent into the Beijing Airport. The massive urban sprawl was numbing in its size and expanse, stretching to the horizon in every direction, blurred through the fumes of heavy traffic and the smoke of millions of back-yard morning breakfast fires, as another day in China unfolded as it had for a millennium past.

China, a land so ancient that every modern advance seemed swallowed in the timeless rhythms of another epoch, beckoned to the jet-lagged travelers with a wisdom and serenity born of endless suffering and endless acceptance. A land so vast there was no way these travelers could absorb where they had suddenly arrived, like visitors transported to a faraway planet. China swept over them, and they surrendered before it, awed by its eternal majesty, its bent and broken poverty, and the dignity and quiet compassion of its myriad citizens whose names and lives, hopes, and dreams could only be counted and kept by their Creator.

Monica, Jean, Edward, and Alex stood bleary-eyed and half asleep midway down a long line leading through customs. The smell of coal smoke clung to their nostrils, and every surface of the grimy airport seemed worn away with constant use. Caught between a feudal way of life and an industrial and technological revolution, China was balanced, as well, between the First World and the Third World, a sleeping giant only now rousing itself to wakefulness.

As they approached the kiosks of the customs officers, Monica could feel the tension growing in Jean's body, expressed most clearly in her white knuckles wrapped around her passport. "Don't worry," Monica said with a reassuring touch. "You'll do fine." She hoped the words would do more to buoy her friend than they were doing for her. Their journey, her mission, and the purpose they had set out upon could be thwarted by one overzealous bureaucrat. As the line lurched forward, the angel promised herself she wasn't going to let that happen. No matter what.

Up ahead, the queue split in two directions, the first toward a sign that read *Chinese Nationals,* the other toward one printed with the words *All Others.* As Jean took her place alone in the first line, Monica sent her off with another smile. "See you on the other side," she whispered.

She watched as Jean approached a middle-aged man in uniform who opened her passport and began to study it carefully, shifting from its pages to Jean's face and back again. He snapped at her with rapid-fire questions, and the young woman's face went slack with fear. It's now or never, thought Monica and, with an inspiration born of desperation, she let out a piercing yelp and dropped her suitcase onto the floor, making sure, in the process, that the latch came undone.

From out of the valise a strange and colorful assortment of novelty items and toys spilled onto the floor. Toys and gadgets, thingamajigs and whatnots went skittering into every corner of the crowded lobby. Several of the more outrageous samples—a set of chattering teeth, a mechanical duck, and several toy soldiers, began to march off in all directions.

"Oh my goodness!" cried Monica, doing her best imitation of an absent-minded klutz. "How embarrassing!" She turned to the customs official who stood, his mouth agape, watching the chaotic spectacle. "You see," she explained, fluttering her hands, "I'm in the toy business! I'm on a business trip, and this is my sample case! Excuse me," she said, interrupting herself to tap the man in front of her, an Indian businessman in a turban. "Would you mind grabbing those chattering teeth before they get away? Oh, dear. There goes my duck! I'm terribly sorry!"

Having created a distraction on a grand scale, the angel was more than a little pleased with her performance, noting with satisfaction the effect it had on its intended audience. From across the room, the customs officer examining Jean's passport was leaning out of his cubicle, staring with fascination at the sight of runaway toys marching mindlessly across the line that marked official entry into the nation of China. Still staring, he absently stamped Jean's passport and waved her on.

With a sigh of relief, Jean moved through the line with a barely perceptible nod in Monica's direction. The angel, busy scrambling after her toys, winked back. Still in line, Edward caught the exchange and smiled—the first hurdle had been cleared.

Behind him, however, Alex was watching Monica's antics with disapproval. "Maybe we made a mistake with her," he noted dubiously to his boss, but Edward just shook his head. "She'll do just fine," he replied.

Monica, meanwhile, was stuffing the last of her wayward toys back into the suitcase. She cast a look across the crowded arrivals lounge for the missing mechanical duck when suddenly, from behind, someone reached out to hand her the toy. She turned. It was Andrew.

"Thank you," she said to her fellow angel.

"My pleasure." Andrew smiled back and together they walked down a long hallway into the gray light of a Beijing morning. Andrew's unexpected presence left a lingering question in Monica's mind. Was the Angel of Death on a vacation to Asia? Or was this official business?

Chapter Nine

On the taxi ride from the airport to the hotel, each of the four passengers registered a different impression of the passing cityscape. For Jean, the flood of memories and emotions took hold of her as she was carried through the crowded streets, back to a past she never thought she would revisit.

For Monica, the marvel of the Eastern world was tempered by the sense of oppression that seemed to hang in the air like the heavy smoke of the cooking fires from the sidewalk food stands. This is a land where the yearning for freedom is so great it's like a hunger, she thought.

For Edward, the passing parade was simply a

backdrop to the focused attention he had turned
on Jean. What must she be thinking? he wondered. What must she be feeling?

And for Alex, each anonymous face passing
by the taxi window was a potential customer for
a Tanner toy. We've hit the mother lode, he
thought to himself, with profit margins dancing
nimbly in his mind.

The taxi pulled off into a neighborhood of
Western-style high-rises and block-long facades
of luxury shops and exclusive apartment com-
plexes, coming to a stop at the front entrance of
a well-appointed hotel, its lobby trimmed in a
chrome-and-gold motif that would have done
justice to any Park Avenue or Rodeo Drive address.
A phalanx of bellhops and doormen rushed to
the cab as they arrived, then followed them
through the wide revolving doors with armfuls
of luggage. Inside, Chinese businessmen in expen-
sively tailored suits chatted on cell phones while
their wives browsed the well-stocked windows
of the hotel shopping arcade.

"It's amazing," marveled Jean. "It's all changed
so much."

"Five-star hotels," remarked Edward. "Upscale boutiques. Thousands of years of keeping out Western culture—"

"And it only took ten years to turn it into the Upper West Side," snorted Alex.

As they approached the front desk, Alex took Jean aside. "Tell them we're with Tanner Toys," he instructed, "and that we've got four suites reserved."

"We've been expecting you," said the haughty front desk clerk in impeccable, British-inflected English before Jean could translate. "I'll have the bellman show you to your rooms immediately. Oh," he added, "and I have a message for a Mr. Tanner."

"That's me," said Edward.

"In that case," said the clerk with a frosty smile, "there's a Mr. Wu waiting for you at the bar."

At the mention of the name, a jolt of anticipation ran through Edward, Monica, and, especially, Jean, as if they had been suddenly connected to an electric current. It was a feeling with no name, but only the wordless certainty that they were all moving closer to the fulfillment of a preordained destiny. With nothing said among them, all three began to move across the lobby to the bar, with a puzzled Alex bringing up the rear.

In the deep, rich shadows of the leather-upholstered bar, a well-dressed Chinese man, young but with an aura of serious purpose about him, sat alone at a far table. As the foursome approached, he rose to greet them, extending his hand in the Western style.

"Mr. Tanner?" he asked Edward in well-practiced English.

"Mr. Wu?" responded Edward.

"Yes," the man replied. "But, please, call me George."

Edward took a step back as if he had been slapped in the face. That destiny they had sensed had suddenly taken a giant step forward, and coincidence was simply no longer an option.

Unaware of the impact his name had imparted, George smiled and continued. "Forgive me," he said with a slight bow. "I know it's presumptuous. But I thought I'd invite you to dinner on behalf of Liberty Moon International Management before we sat down for business tomorrow."

"Of course," murmured Edward, still trying to recover from his shock. He turned to the others. "I'd like to introduce my associate, Mr. Alex Stella. Monica here is our trade consultant and"—he took a deep breath—"this is our interpreter . . . Jean Chang."

It was George's turn now to stop and stare and try his best to cover his amazement. Jean stepped forward, her face alight with seeing her old friend, alive and well once again, and carrying with him, perhaps, news of her daughter. But her smile abruptly faded as George's scowl warned her away. He turned to Edward. "I am sorry," he said in a strained voice. "Sometimes my English is weak. Please allow me to speak in Chinese for a moment."

"Of course," answered Edward, intently watching the unspoken struggle between the reunited friends. A rapid-fire exchange in Chinese followed, with Jean asking urgent questions and George giving clipped and, to Edward and Monica's ears, almost hostile responses until with a sudden, imperious gesture, he cut her off. Jean stepped back, a stunned look on her face.

"I am so sorry," said George stiffly to Edward. "My plans have changed. I will be unable to take you to dinner tonight. In fact, I am no longer certain that we can do business together." He bowed now with full Chinese protocol, his former friendliness vanished. "Perhaps we will meet again, someday. Excuse me." He hurried off. Jean turned away, hiding her brimming tears in the shadows of the deeper recesses of the dimly lit bar.

"What's with that guy?" demanded the mystified Alex. "He knew her. It was plain as day. This is just great." He threw up his hands. "One hour in the most populated country in the world, and our translator runs in to an old boyfriend."

"Maybe you should head up to your room," Edward suggested. "We can sort this out later."

"Good idea," replied Alex and slouched out of the bar and back to the lobby.

As soon as he had moved out of sight, Edward and Monica turned to Jean, the same question forming on their lips, a question Jean answered before they could ask.

"That was George," she insisted, "but he says

he doesn't know who I am." She choked back a fresh flood of tears. "And he's never heard of my daughter."

"But how can that be?" asked Edward in disbelief. "How could he just lie like that?"

"He is afraid," said Jean, and her voice rang with certainty. "I could see it in his eyes. He is very afraid."

The fear that Jean had seen in her old friend's eyes drove George down the crowded streets outside the hotel as if he were being pursued by the demons of an old Chinese ghost story. He turned the corner of a side street where the glittering storefronts of the city's Western-styled district abruptly ended and small apartment blocks and single family homes of an older Beijing neighborhood came into view. Only then did George allow himself to slow down, to finally catch his breath. He tried to understand how the past, with all its frightening echoes of lost hopes and shattered lives, had suddenly intruded into the present. Muttering to himself and shaking his head in futile denial, George wove his way through a rickety marketplace and past the steps of a deserted shrine.

He didn't notice the two angels who stood on the steps, watching him as he passed. Of course, neither did anyone else in the busy little square. Tess and Monica were invisible, their conversation a silent exchange between two beings for whom time and space did not always matter.

"Things are not always what they seem to be in the old country," Tess was advising her charge. "Take George here, for example. He certainly looks like the perfect example of the new China, the one its leaders want the world to see. He's a modern businessman, with his cell phone and his little beeper, ready to cut a deal, twenty-four seven. But to achieve all that, he had to turn his back on his past. And his past just caught up with him."

"He says he doesn't even know Jean," Monica said softly.

"Oh," replied Tess with a sad smile, "he knows

her, all right. He knows her very well. And he also knows what a courageous thing she has just done by returning here. But if he's going to help her, he'll need to find his own courage. And, well, he just doesn't think he's got any to spare."

They watched with timeless eyes as George turned a corner and continued to wander aimlessly through the twisted streets of the old district. Hands behind his back, eyes to the ground, the young man was so sunk in the despair of his own thoughts that he hardly noticed when his feet brought him to the border of an exquisite Chinese garden, set like a jewel in the midst of the grimy city. A voice, gentle but insistent, called to him from near an arched bridge over a pond where koi fish swam lazily.

"Excuse me," said the voice, and George turned to see a large and robust black woman with a striking head of salt-and-pepper colored hair waving at him.

"Do you speak English?" Tess asked, and for the first time, he noticed she was carrying a guide book.

"Yes, I do," he replied, his natural courtesy

overcoming his self-absorption. "May I help you?"

"Well, maybe," Tess answered. "I was wondering what the name of this garden might be."

George looked around, recognizing where he was for the first time. "This is called the Garden of Peaceful Memories," he told the angel.

Tess smiled and nodded. "Peaceful memories. Now, that's beautiful. I guess you'd have to plant pretty early to grow a crop of memories like those, wouldn't you say?"

"I suppose so," George replied, beginning to move away.

"We can't do much about today's flowers," Tess continued, and something in her voice brought him to a halt. "But wouldn't it be something if we could plant some peaceful memories for next season?"

"Yes," said George, surprised at how this strange woman's words stirred something inside him, something that caused his fear to begin to fall away. "Yes, it would."

"Well," Tess cheerfully concluded, "see you around." And with that she was gone, leaving

George to ponder the picture she had planted in his mind . . . a harvest of beautiful memories, that needed to be planted now to be reaped in due season.

Chapter Ten

That same afternoon, Edward took advantage of Jean's hometown status to ask for a tour of Beijing's historic sights—as much to take her mind off her troubling encounter with George as to actually play the tourist in one of the most fascinating cities in the world.

But what started out as a whirlwind trip past the landmarks and monuments of the Chinese capital soon took a more personal turn as Jean, almost without realizing it, began circling closer and closer to the neighborhood where she and Gus had lived and where they had raised Piao Yue for those few precious years.

So it was that the pair found themselves in a part of town rarely visited by outsiders, as the afternoon light threw deep shadows across the uneven streets and the peeling paint on the doors of run-down apartment buildings. Around them, vendors sleepily tended their wares in small carts and kiosks, while housewives went about their daily rituals and children played together as children everywhere do, spinning fun from the simplest scraps found in the streets and gutters. Somewhere far off, a dog barked, its mournful baying blending with the tuneless singing of an old man sitting at an open window. For all the apparent poverty of the little street, there was a peace here, the calm unraveling of a day like any other day.

"This is my old alley," Jean was telling Edward as they strolled down the street. "I know it's not the most exciting part of the city—"

"Please—" countered Edward. "Don't worry. I'm interested in seeing it. After your story, I almost feel as if I've been here."

Jean smiled gratefully. "They call these tiny streets hutongs," she explained. "This one is called the Hutong of Yellow Canaries because, long ago, such birds were kept here." She stopped in front of a nondescript doorway. "And this," she said, "is—was—my home."

Together they opened the door and, walking down a dim hallway, emerged onto a courtyard around which two stories of cramped apartments had been built. Edward was only too aware of the feelings that Jean was trying to contain. He could sense them radiating from her as she looked around the small, open space: waves of tender sorrow too intense for this confined place.

"Here Piao Yue played with the neighbor's kitten," she explained, pointing to a stoop at one end of the courtyard. "And over there, Gus would sit and write his poetry when the sun was shining."

"Your husband was a poet and a sculptor?"

She nodded. "Yes. He was very creative." Then, suddenly, she remembered something and, crossing over to an alcove in the wall, searched out a particular board. Looking to see that they were alone, she pried it off, revealing a small enclosure. Reaching inside, she pulled out a plastic bag and, opening it, produced a tattered journal.

She showed it almost proudly to Edward, a relic from a former life that proved she had once lived and loved in this very place. "I'd nearly forgotten," she explained. "We always kept copies here, in case we were searched." Opening the precious booklet, she began to read, halting occasionally to transpose the words from Chinese to English.

"She is funny to watch," she read in a soft voice Edward strained to hear, "my little girl. She . . . toddles along the hutong. Will she go here? Will she go there? She . . . plops down on her bottom. She screams with delight. She will go wherever she likes. She will cry with a happy voice any word that comes to her mind. How long will it last, this childhood of Liberty Moon?" Jean began to weep, openly and unashamedly— for herself, for her daughter, for her suffering country. "What must I do to save China?"

Without even thinking, acting only from a tender and compassionate urge that felt at once familiar and long-absent, Edward reached for

Jean and held her to him, wanting only to still the sobs that shuddered through her delicate frame. "You are the bravest person I know," he said as he wiped her tears away. She turned to look up into his eyes, where his tears, too, had begun to form. They lingered there for a long moment in the courtyard, gazing at one another, while other feelings, new and exhilarating feelings, began to take shape in their hearts. At another time, in another place, they might have kissed. But now was not that time, and here was not that place, and from that recognition their intimacy faded, like the sunlight fading around them. Jean gently disengaged herself, pulling back and drying her eyes.

"We had better go," she said. "It is getting late. Mr. Stella will be waiting for us."

Night was coming on quickly as Edward and Jean arrived back at the hotel where, indeed, Alex Stella was waiting for them, tapping his foot and impatiently checking his wrist watch.

"Where have you two been?" he demanded.

"Jean took me on a tour," Edward replied equitably. "What's the problem?"

"Only that the nut we met this afternoon called back," snapped Alex.

"You mean . . . George?" Jean tremulously asked.

"You got it," replied Alex. "Anyway, he wants to meet us right away. Says he's got some property that's perfect for our new factory." Shooting a look at his watch he began to move toward the lobby doors. "Come on. We've got an appointment in forty-five minutes."

The factory building squatted in a rusty industrial park on the outskirts of the city, surrounded by the belching smokestacks of a steel plant and several other cavernous manufacturing concerns—some deserted, some still operating. Lit by the gas fires of a refinery and echoing with the metallic clangs of heavy industry, there was a haunted, uninhabited feel to the place as the foursome pulled up in a taxi. Not only were they far off the tourist track now, but far away from the

Beijing even most Chinese saw. This was a no-man's-land, a blighted monument to the government's drive to modernize, no matter what the cost to the citizens or the environment.

Standing forlornly in the parking lot of the factory as the taxi pulled away, they wondered for a moment if they had come to the wrong place, when, from a side door near the loading dock, the figure of George emerged and hurried up to them.

"I am so glad you could come," he said, careful to avoid looking in Jean's direction. "This place was added to our list at the last moment, and I wanted you to see it right away. I believe it is quite suitable for our joint venture."

"I thought you said we couldn't do business," said Edward looking the young businessman straight in the eye.

"Please," pleaded George as he led the way toward the looming factory gates. "Forgive me. I had heard some . . . upsetting news. Something personal. But it is all right now. Everything is . . . how do you say? . . . 'A-OK'."

Pushing open the door, George escorted them

into the vast and empty building, littered with the debris of a previous enterprise. From the rafters high above they could hear pigeons cooing, and the lurid light from the gas burn-off outside cast wicked shadows over the looming walls.

"One moment, please," said George as he opened an electric panel on the wall and switched on a bank of lights. The factory floor was now bathed in a pale fluorescent wash, the glow draining their faces of color. "This is an older building, of course," George explained, "but the state is willing to renovate it to your special require—"

His sales pitch was suddenly interrupted by a loud clattering that sent its echoes bouncing off the high walls with deafening resonance. The chain that hoisted the loading dock door rattled as the corrugated metal began to rise and a group of spectral figures shuffled onto the factory floor. Shielding her eyes from the glare of an outside spotlight, Monica could just make out the slumped shoulders and slow, painful gait of the new arrivals. She could also see several men standing to one side, moving the others in with the butts of their automatic weapons.

As she watched, one of the soldiers looked in their direction and, with a sharp exclamation, pointed his rifle at them and began to move in their direction, brandishing his weapon and shouting incomprehensible commands.

George moved quickly to intercept the approaching soldier, talking loudly and pointing to a sheaf of papers on his clipboard. Everyone else in the factory had frozen in place as the agitated conversation continued. Monica could see for the first time that the group of men on the loading dock were bound together with chains at their wrists and ankles.

"What's going on here?" Edward was asking Jean.

"The soldier is asking what we are doing here," Jean explained, translating rapidly. "George is saying we are here on business to look at the factory, but the soldier says that it is impossible . . . that no foreigners are allowed here. George is telling him that there must be some mistake. He has authorization."

A mistake, Monica thought to herself as the argument continued. Is it a mistake or is there another reason we're here? What purpose are we meant to fulfill?

Tuning back into Jean's ongoing translation, Monica heard her explain that while George was loudly insisting that they were allowed to visit the facility, the soldier was insisting that no one could enter until the renovation was complete.

In the meantime, the chained men on the dock moved slowly into the factory where another soldier unlinked them and gave them orders to begin clearing the rubbish off the floor. Dazed and drooping, the men obeyed, walking like robots through the deep shadows cast by the harsh fluorescent light.

"What're they saying now?" Alex urged Jean, who was still listening to the heated exchange between George and the officer.

"The soldier says that this area is strictly off-limits until the . . . prisoners . . . have finished their work." She stopped, as all four realized for the first time what might be happening in front of their eyes. "This must be a work detail . . . from a prison camp," Jean whispered.

"Those are prisoners?" asked Edward.

"They're using criminals to do the work?" Alex questioned.

"Not criminals like you'd imagine," Monica answered. "These are prisoners from a 'reeducation camp,' people who have offended the government in some way."

"But this is outrageous—" began Alex before Edward silenced him with a wave of his hand. He was carefully watching George, who was pulling out a carton of cigarettes from his briefcase. Then reaching into his jacket pocket, George produced a fistful of crisp American bills, which he slipped into the box of cigarettes and set down carefully at the feet of the soldier. The uniformed man barked out a command, and bowing low, George backed away, returning to them without once taking his eyes off the ground.

"What is going on?" Alex demanded.

"We have five minutes," replied George, "to complete our inspection."

"Look, you tell the warden there, or whatever

he is, that—" Alex's tirade was interrupted by a sudden gasp from Jean. The sound billowed up into the factory like a cry of despair that might be heard to the gates of heaven.

"Jean!" said Monica, alarmed. "What is it?"

Jean pointed to one of the ghostly figures, rolling a half-empty oil barrel across the floor with slow and deliberate movements. "That man," Jean said, turning to Monica with a look that somehow brought hope and horror together. "That man is Gus . . . my husband!"

Chapter Eleven

Gus! Monica's racing mind grabbed hold of the name. Yes, of course. That's why we've come to this place.

Even as the stunning revelation sank in, across the factory floor Gus stumbled and fell as he struggled to move the heavy barrel onto the loading dock. As he fell to his knees, Jean stifled a cry of agony as if she, too, felt her own body give way, and Monica moved quickly to her side.

"There are many, many things that have brought you and your husband to this moment, Jean," she urgently whispered. "But you can't waste a minute now asking why or how. You've got to hurry. You don't have much time."

As if in a dream, Jean nodded and began walking toward Gus, oblivious to the danger of the heavily armed guards around him. Edward and Monica watched her with bated breath, while an outraged Alex blustered at the embarrassed George.

"Do you mean to tell me that they're using prison labor to secure an export agreement?" he demanded, using his best attorney's tactics. "May I remind you, Mr. Wu, that such exploitation has been outlawed by at least a half dozen international treaties?"

"Yes, I know," George replied, weighing his words carefully. "And officially, this is not happening. We do not belong here, and what we have seen we were not meant to see. It was a mistake. A mistake that can only last a little longer."

"We understand," was Edward's terse reply as he registered the implication of George's words and turned back to the grim scene unfolding on the far side of the factory, where Jean's inexorable journey to her husband continued.

As Jean came closer, Gus struggled back to his feet and began the seemingly endless task of rolling the rusting barrel. Nearby, a guard barked an order to the other prisoners and, as if compelled by some invisible force, they melted away, drawing back until Gus stood alone, his shoulders hunched over his dreary labor. Pushing the barrel a few more feet, he once again stumbled and fell, and the tears that filled his eyes were as much from the hopeless despair of his plight as from the pain and exhaustion of his depleted and emaciated body.

So sunk into despondency was the prisoner that at first he didn't notice the figure standing over him or hear her gentle voice calling out his name. It wasn't until Jean kneeled beside him and held his thin, pale face in her hands that Gus understood for the first time that he was in the middle of a true miracle.

Ignoring his rotting teeth and gray skin covered with sores, Jean covered his face with kisses, then took his cracked and bleeding hands and put them to her own face, kissing his palms and pressing his dirty fingers against her cheeks. For a moment, no words passed between them, and none were needed. The look in their eyes expressed everything they felt . . . and more. The love that still burned, the sorrow of separation, the longing that had never died . . . a lifetime passed in the space of a few precious moments.

When at last Gus opened his mouth and tried to form a sentence, it was clear that he had not spoken, or been spoken to, for a very long time.

"Is it really you?" he said, his voice brittle and broken.

"Yes, my dearest," Jean answered as her tears covered the hands she still held to her face. "It's really me."

"Have I died?" Gus asked, in wonder and awe. "Or have I come back to life?"

"Shh . . . ," Jean quieted him. "I am the one who has been dead all these years."

"And the baby?" Gus hardly dared to ask. The darkness that passed over his wife's face told him the answer. They held each other tightly, weeping together for their lost daughter.

Monica, watching from a distance, shed tears of her own as she witnessed the heartbreaking reunion, while George and Edward talked softly, off to one side.

"It is very unusual for me to get such incorrect information," George was saying, while behind his words it was only too easy for Edward to pick up on the truth of what was unfolding— George had arranged for Jean and Gus to see each other once again, at what must have been great personal risk to himself.

"Do all the prisoners have the same history?" he asked, playing along with George's elaborate ruse.

The businessman shook his head. "No." He pointed across the factory to Gus. "That one, for example, was arrested for crimes against the state after the student incidents of 1989. He spent three years in prison and then was arrested immediately after his release for disclosing state secrets."

"How can you get ahold of state secrets in prison?" asked Edward.

George looked at him with an expression that seemed to sum up the gulf between their two worlds. "He was overheard describing the conditions he lived under," was his deadpan reply.

From the open port of the loading dock came the sound of an approaching truck, followed by a volley of loud voices and slamming doors. George turned to shout a quick warning to Jean and Gus, who pulled apart and looked deeply into each other's eyes for what might well be the last time.

"You must go," Gus urged his wife.

"No!" Jean's voice was edged with desperation. "I don't care. I won't lose you. Not again!"

Gus took her by the shoulders and for a moment, the strength and resolve of another man—a man unbroken by tragedy and terror—shone through his eyes and brought a firm tone to his voice. "I was never lost," he told her. "We have always been together, we have always been one. It is time now to move on. I will not live very much longer—"

"No!" Jean cried, denying his words with all her heart.

"Listen!" he insisted in a fierce whisper. "And never forget. Freedom never comes without sacrifice. I died for China . . . but I lived . . . for you!"

His words echoed through the empty factory, and Jean felt her heart fluttering in her chest as the passion of her husband's declaration brought back in a rush the life and love they had once shared together.

"Forever," Jean said as she fell into the deep pools of his dark eyes.

"Forever." Gus nodded, as he, too, lost himself in her gaze.

From across the factory George called out again, but Monica was already at Jean's side, pulling her to her feet and helping her back as her cries of anguish echoed throughout the empty expanse. A soldier's brutal order, the shuffling feet of the prisoners moving into place, and as Gus moved along with the group, suddenly the impact of the moment hit and Jean shouted his name in a voice that tore at Monica's heart.

The soldiers escorting the prison detail stopped where they were and snapped to attention. At first it was difficult to tell, from where Monica and the others stood, if it was Jean's heartrending sobs that had brought them up short, until another man, a superior officer by the look of his stature and uniform, entered through the loading dock door. A brief, huddled conference ensued between the colonel and the guard who had spoken to George, after which they both arrogantly walked over to them, the officer's eyes darting among their faces as if he could see all their secrets revealed there.

"Edward . . . ?" said Alex uncertainly.

"Keep quiet!" was the preemptory reply.

With a jerk of his head, the soldier instructed George to hand over his clipboard to the officer, who cast a skeptical gaze at its list of factories and authorization forms. "American business?" he asked in a clipped voice, and George nodded as the officer's gaze turned toward Jean.

He squinted at her, trying to reach some troubling question in the back of his mind and, sensing the jeopardy of the moment, George cleared his throat and with a loud voice said, "We have made a terrible mistake, I am afraid. You may rest assured that someone at my office shall be punished for causing such confusion. And now, if you will excuse us—" He herded the others toward the door, moving quickly and not daring to look back.

But Jean, as if commanded by something deep

inside her, could not help but turn for a last look at Gus as he moved with the other prisoners into the back of the waiting truck. He smiled and nodded even as the guard used the butt of his rifle to shove him along.

Hurrying to catch up with the others as they headed toward a pair of waiting cars, Jean pulled George aside. "Thank you, George," she said in a low voice. "When can we talk together? When can you tell me the truth?"

George cast a quick, nervous look over his shoulder. The colonel stood on the loading dock, watching them go. "Forgive me, Miss Chang," George said stiffly. "But I have no idea what you are talking about. Please"—he gestured—"this car is at your disposal. I must return to my office. I suggest you tell no one of this visit. As you know," he added with a hard and knowing look, "there is no word for privacy in Chinese."

With that, he was through the door of one of the waiting cars, leaving a confused, sorrowful, and suddenly very lonely Jean to wonder what she should do next and to whom she might turn for help.

Chapter Twelve

The car that had driven Edward, Alex, Monica, and Jean from the overwhelming revelations at the factory sat idling at the edge of a park in the central district of Beijing, not far from the hotel. Both the park and the streets around it were deserted at this late hour, but nevertheless, the foursome kept their voices low as they spoke together. The feeling of being watched, of not knowing who, or what, was around the next corner, had settled on all of them like a dull headache. It was the consequence of being thrust suddenly into a society where freedom was only a word, and betrayal was celebrated as a virtue by a government that could never be held to account by the very people it ruled.

Alex, nearly apoplectic, was having the hardest time of all keeping his voice to a whisper, as Edward, for the first time, filled his friend in on the whole story. What came out of the lawyer's mouth, instead, was a hissing stream of uncomprehending questions, as he paced back and forth over the cobblestone path.

"Chinese dissidents?" he said incredulously. "Missing children? Tiananmen Square? Edward! Have you lost your mind? This is your business you're putting on the line here. Your livelihood . . . and mine!"

"I know that, Alex."

"We've been friends for twenty years," Alex continued as if he hadn't heard. "And you're doing this to me?" He pointed at Jean. "For her?"

"Her name is Jean," Edward replied evenly.

"I don't care what her name is!" Alex hissed. "You've put us all in danger! They could kick us out." He shook his head in exasperation. "The whole world is trying to get these people out, and we bring one of them back in?"

Edward, unruffled by his friend's tirade, turned to Monica. "Now that's an idea," he said. "Maybe we could get one of those human rights organizations to help us get Gus out."

"Us!" shouted the outraged Alex, no longer caring who might hear. "Us?" In a frenzy of frustration he gave a vicious dropkick to the briefcase he held in his hands, scattering papers like snowflakes over the ground. Then, for all the world like a little boy throwing a temper tantrum, he stomped on the documents, stirring them up into the breeze and spreading them even farther down the path.

Edward and the others waited patiently for him to exhaust himself and, suddenly realizing what he was doing, he began stuffing the soiled papers back into his case, muttering and fuming the whole time.

"You," he said to Jean, looking up from where he crouched on the park's damp ground. "You're outta here. Did you see the way that colonel, or whatever he was, looked at you? He knows there's something screwy going on here. As soon as he figures out who you are, and how you got here, we're cooked."

Monica stepped forward, her eyes flashing anger. "Mr. Stella," she said, fighting hard to contain herself. "It seems to me that if you have no place in your heart for what happened here today; if you can't see that there is no business more important than a human life or a restored family; if none of that matters to you, then forgive me for saying that you're already 'cooked.'"

"And you, lady," Alex shot back, "are fired."

"No, she's not," Edward interjected in the same even tone. He was obviously used to his friend's outbursts.

"Edward . . . please," Alex said, with an utterly bewildered look on his face.

"Mr. Stella is right," said Jean, stepping forward for the first time. There was something about the calm and completely focused tone of her voice that drew and held the others' attention. "To try to help my husband now would only further endanger his life." She turned to Edward, favoring him with a warm smile that, once again, stirred some long-dormant feelings deep in his heart. "And it would endanger you as well, Mr. Tanner. Gus is simply too sick to survive the anger of the men who put him in prison. It is best that we try to continue our work and forget everything that has happened today."

"But, Jean," said Monica in alarm. "What about your little girl?"

Jean turned her smile to the angel. "We must be patient," she said. "I have found George. He has found my husband. When it is time, when it is safe . . . perhaps he will tell me where I can find her, as well."

"It's settled, then," said Edward, already moving back to the car. "We stay. All of us."

Jean and Monica followed, but Alex lingered for a moment before joining the others. His frustration and anger had turned now to a cold realization . . . these women had come between him and his best friend. It was a coldness that, once it had touched him, would spread inexorably over his heart and mind.

The next few days were a welter of activity as the representatives from Tanner Toys met with a parade of hopeful Chinese entrepreneurs, all angling for a piece of the fabled American profit pie. It was early on a sunny and unseasonably warm Beijing afternoon that the foursome were finally concluding their meeting with the last of their business contacts in the plush lobby of the hotel.

"Thank you very much," Edward was saying, putting to use the practice he had gotten into of bowing. He was getting the hang of it. "You have put together an exceptionally impressive presentation, and you can be sure we will give it serious consideration."

As he spoke, Jean rattled off a simultaneous translation, while the Chinese businessmen all smiled and bowed back. "Tell them thanks for lunch," added Alex. "And especially those delicious crunchy things."

"Those were fried chicken feet," Monica informed him.

Alex made a face. "Thanks," he said. "That's a little more than I needed to know."

As the men made their way across the crowded lobby, Alex rubbed his hands with satisfaction. "Now we're getting somewhere," he chortled as they walked to the front desk and to retrieve their room keys. "These guys could be the ones . . ."

"Liberty Moon's offer was better organized and more generous," Monica reminded him.

"No way, José," Alex retorted. "Too many strings attached to that one." He threw a look in Jean's direction. "If you know what I mean."

When the arrived at the desk a familiar figure was also waiting for the desk clerk. He picked up his key and placed a folded newspaper down on the counter. "Thanks very much," he said to the clerk and turned to the others with a smile. "Here's a New York paper, in case anyone wants to read it."

Monica turned and with a slight tilt of her head, acknowledged Andrew. It was the first time she had seen him since their arrival at customs, but she had a feeling it wouldn't be the last during this trip.

Edward, meanwhile, had picked up the newspaper and was scanning the headlines. Monica sighed. "It's too bad," she said to him, returning to the business at hand. "Liberty Moon's a solid company."

"Sure," said Edward, still riffling through the paper. "But George must have known his chances with us were over the minute he showed us that prison labor detail. He would never be able to work with us now . . . not without sending up a big red flag . . . no pun intended."

Monica turned to Jean. It was the first time they had even brought up the events of that fateful night since it had happened. "Has George given you any hint about what might have happened to Piao Yue?" she asked delicately.

Jean shook her head. The subject was obviously a painful one. "Not yet," she replied. "He must know where she is. But please understand. I do not blame him for being careful. It is different here. Sometimes it is safer to know nothing."

"Monica," said Edward, and the ominous ring in his voice caused both of them to turn in his direction.

Edward was holding open the newspaper and, folding it in half, handed it over to the angel, as he pointed out a small item on a back page. She read the headline with dread, hoping against hope it wouldn't tell her what she already knew. "Missing Dissident Dies in Prison" the headline announced, and Monica quickly folded over the paper and tucked it under her arm until she could decide when and how to break the news to Jean. Across the lobby she saw Andrew as he made his way out the door. She knew now why he had been sent, and her sudden sadness was softened by knowing that Gus had been escorted to a far better place than he had ever known.

Chapter Thirteen

$\mathcal{J}$ean, Edward, and Monica sat alone in the bar, empty now of all of its happy tourists and anxious businessmen. An eerie calm seemed to have descended over the whole hotel, with only a few stragglers seated in the comfortable chairs and sofas, reading newspapers in a dozen different languages and lost in the thoughts all travelers share at the end of the day.

Spread out before them was a pile of some of those same international newspapers they had already thumbed through in search of a corroborant account of Gus's death. Monica was now reading out loud, her voice solemn and subdued as she recounted the tragic tale.

"The official Chinese news agency," she read, "acknowledged that Zhang Xaio Gang, long considered a victim of Tiananmen Square's 1989 three-day massacre, in fact spent most of the last nine years in prison. The government also reports that Zhang renounced his participation in the democracy movement before expiring from natural causes. He was thirty-five."

She shared a moment of silence with the others, as if out of respect for the fallen warrior of freedom.

It was Edward who broke the silence. "The clerk told me the Hong Kong newspapers weren't delivered today," he said.

"Well, now we know why," Monica observed. "They probably carried the story, too."

"Not the true story," Jean said with anger but no bitterness. "Gus would never have said those things. They can't keep telling lies. I won't let them."

"No one believes it, Jean," Edward said, putting his hand over hers as he had done so long ago in a little Chinese restaurant halfway around the world. So much had happened since then, and Edward, remembering the moment, felt a special closeness to Jean, along with a worried concern for her future.

"He knew he was dying," Jean continued. "He told me never to forget what he was dying for. But you know something? I had forgotten. For years, I've felt such shame, such anger that we failed in our struggle and that so many had to die for that failure. I believed only that we had been young and foolish and that we didn't know what we were doing. But when I saw him again that night I remembered. I remembered that there are some things worth dying for. I'd almost forgotten that . . . until I saw his face one more time . . . for the last time. And then it all came back. I shall always be thankful for that miracle."

"Yes," Monica agreed. "It was a miracle."

Suddenly Alex appeared beside them, his face pale.

"Alex?" asked Edward. "What's the problem?"

"Don't turn around," Alex answered in a barely audible voice. "And don't make any sudden moves. Some soldiers just came to my room. I'm not sure what they were saying, but I've got a pretty good idea it was about Jean. They had some old picture of her."

Edward craned his neck around his friend and peered through the doors of the bar to the front desk. Sure enough, a group of soldiers was gathered there, with one of them handing over something to the desk clerk.

Monica immediately read the look on his face and turned to Jean. "Stand up very slowly and walk with me," she said. "Alex and Edward . . . just keep talking."

The two men did their best to act casual as Monica and Jean moved across the bar toward a rear door. But it was too late. In the lobby, one of the soldiers turned in time to catch a glimpse of Jean and alerted his superior with a sharp cry.

"Run," said Edward in a voice at once measured and insistent. "Now!"

Jean did not have to be told twice. Without looking back she raced to the door and, pushing it open, burst into the hotel kitchen. Within seconds the soldiers were pounding across the lobby and into the bar, hot on her trail.

The busy, brightly lit kitchen was instantly plunged into chaos as Jean shoved her way through the cooks and waiters. The squad of soldiers followed a moment later and, instantly, the shouts and protests were silenced as the staff stood like statues, watching as a systematic search of the premises was undertaken. The officer in charge cornered the head chef and, in a rapid stream of Chinese, demanded to know where the fugitive had gone. Wide-eyed and frightened, but unwilling to play the informer, the chef remained frozen in place until the interrogating officer pointed to the rear door and was met with the chef's vigorous nod. Within moments, the squad had squeezed through the door and fanned out into the alley behind the hotel.

It was then that Edward poked his head inside and, seeing that the coast was clear, signaled for Monica to follow him into the kitchen. The workers resumed their chores as if nothing had happened, trying their best to ignore the foreigners who stood in their midst. Edward's eyes roamed the gleaming stainless steel expanse until his eyes fell on a cupboard door under the sink. With a quick smile to Monica he crossed and opened it, fully expecting to find Jean in her accustomed hiding place. But the smile faded, replaced by a look of worry and puzzlement as the opened cupboard revealed a space empty of everything but a few cans of cleanser and a lone plumber's helper. He turned to Monica, the look in his eyes close to panic, and the angel felt her own rush of trepidation. So much sorrow . . . so much tragedy. How many more would have to die before this mission came to an end?

It was a question she wanted badly to put to Andrew when, later that afternoon, she met with her fellow angels at the Garden of Peaceful Memories. They were sitting in a gazebo close to the spot where Tess had prompted George to listen to his heart and act on his convictions.

The trio sat in silence for a long moment,

listening to the distant sounds of the city beyond the drooping willow trees, each lost in thoughts and prayers that belonged only to them. At last, Monica turned to Andrew and broached the subject that had been on her heart since she had read the dreadful news of Gus's death.

"Why won't you tell me?" she asked him one more time.

Andrew sighed. "I've seen many political prisoners die of 'natural causes' in China, Monica," he explained. "But there's nothing 'natural' about them. Gus died terribly and painfully, and to have to describe such a thing is very hard on me . . . hard on my spirit."

"But you stayed with him?" Monica asked, seeking whatever comfort she could.

"Of course," was Andrew's reply as he put his hand on her shoulder. "And you should know, he died with hope."

"Yes, he did," interjected Tess. "And we need to keep that hope alive. But first we've got to find Jean."

"You mean," responded a puzzled Monica, "you don't know where she is?"

Tess shook her head. "No, baby girl," she answered. "And that's because we're not the ones who are supposed to find her."

"But who is?" asked Monica.

"He's back at the hotel now," Tess replied. "And you'd better hurry back before he misses his chance."

Chapter Fourteen

Edward was packing his suitcase with grim determination when he heard a knock at the door of his room. "It's open," he said without looking up, barely glancing in Monica's direction as she entered.

"Going somewhere?" she asked him softly.

"You know," said Edward, opening a drawer and pulling out a pile of socks and underwear, "when I was in the seventh grade I remember a chapter in my geography book called 'China, Land of Contrasts.' Man, what they don't teach you in school, huh?"

"Edward—" Monica began, only to be cut off by an impatient wave of his hand.

"Spare me," he said curtly. "Alex was right. We don't belong here. There is a plane at eight, if you're interested."

A long silence ensued as Monica watched the executive pile in the last of his clothes and slam shut the lid of his luggage. "What are you afraid of, Edward?" she asked at last.

He looked at her incredulously. "My business going down the tubes," he said, counting the reasons on his fingers. "Imprisonment. Torture. Will that do for starters?"

Monica moved into the room, crossing to him and standing face-to-face, capturing his attention with her eyes. "If you ask me," she countered, "what you're really afraid of is getting truly involved with something besides the bottom line."

Barely controlled rage flashed in Edward's eyes now. "Look," he said, seething, "I'm on to you. I don't know how you worked it exactly, but you're no trade consultant. You're some kind of political activist or something. And you've used me. You've used all of us."

Monica remained calm in the face of Edward's

verbal assault. "That's not why you're angry with me," she told him. "You're angry because I encouraged you to take out your soul and let it fly. You did. And look what happened. All of a sudden that labor pool of 1.2 billion Chinese faces, the ones that all looked alike to you, have become one beautiful individual, whose life suddenly matters. And now you're terrified you'll lose her before you even understand why."

Edward stared at her, the fury draining from his face. The moments passed slowly as her words found their mark deep in that same tender place where Jean's love and courage and devotion had first touched him. Now Monica, too, reached out gently, her fingers resting on his arm. "You can't leave now," she said. "This is what your soul was made for."

There were no more words to say, no more denials to make, no more evasions to try. Edward sighed and snapped open his luggage again. "I'm not much of a hero," he confessed. "I'm the wrong guy to be saving her."

"Maybe she's going to be saving you," replied Monica with a smile.

An hour later, Edward and the angel were wending their way through a crowded Beijing street, while Edward searched desperately for a familiar landmark. A flower seller's stall; a building painted an unusual color of blue; a glimpse of the skyline down a broad avenue . . . suddenly he had his bearings as they turned a corner and made their way down the block of Jean's old neighborhood.

Stopping outside the door to the apartment building they had visited together, he turned to Monica. "I don't know," he said. "I thought, just maybe, there might be a chance—" He stopped, catching sight of a familiar figure across the street. Standing in a doorway, her eyes fixed on them as if her concentration could draw their attention, Jean was huddled, wrapped in an oversized jacket that gave her the anonymous look of a peasant. Her hair disheveled, her face dirty, and her eyes stark with fear, she looked warily around before hurrying over to them across the crowded street. Together, they ducked into the sheltering shadows of the doorway.

"Were you followed?" asked the anxious Jean.

"No," Monica reassured her. "We were very careful."

"I was hoping you'd remember this place," said Jean, turning to Edward with a wan smile.

"Some things you don't forget," he replied.

Jean ducked her head out of the doorway and looked up and down the street. "You shouldn't stay," she warned them. "They'll find you, too."

"Too late," Edward answered as he suddenly felt his heart leap into his throat. His next words came quickly in a rush, faster than he could pull them back or even think about them. "I can't leave. Not without you." He said it again, wanting to make sure that she had heard and understood. "Not without you." Her smile offered him the answer he sought. She knew how he felt. She felt the same way.

Monica, not wanting to interrupt the moment, nonetheless felt the urgency of their situation crowding in on her. "How can we help you?" she asked Jean, who turned to her with a hopeful look dawning on her face.

It was early afternoon, the height of a busy workday, when Edward, Monica, and Jean stepped out of a taxi into an entirely different segment of Beijing life. They moved quickly along a spacious avenue lined with office buildings, where smartly dressed businessmen and their secretaries, decked out in the latest Western fashions, jockeyed for position on the swarming street. As they turned the corner, a sight met them that slowed the hurried pace of all three—a soldier in the middle of the sidewalk was passing out leaflets to the pedestrians, most of whom obediently took what was handed to them, even if they then dropped it a few paces farther on.

Jean reached down and picked up one of the discarded leaflets blown their way in the wake of a passing truck. Her face went pale as she saw what was printed there—her own photo, taken years ago against the backdrop of Tiananmen Square. I look so young, she thought to herself, staring at the pigtailed woman in the simple, padded jacket. So innocent and naïve. They passed by the soldier, trying intensely to appear casual and unconcerned, and safely made it by without being recognized. It was hard not to break into a run as they moved farther down the street, hard to not look back just to make sure they hadn't been spotted. In spite of their fear, Edward paused long enough to scoop up another leaflet and stuff it into his pocket before they moved on.

The threesome moved quickly down the block and ducked into the lobby of a nondescript office building. They moved silently up the stairs until they found the frosted glass door that announced George's business. Entering, they waited patiently for George. Returning from a meeting, still absorbed in a cell phone conversation, George didn't even notice them until he had closed the door and set his briefcase down on the desk. It was then that he saw Edward, silhouetted against the afternoon light that leaked through the blinds of the office window.

"Mr. Tanner," George said, quickly recovering his composure. "I was unaware that we had an appointment."

Edward stepped forward as the light fell from his face, and George turned on a desk lamp to see the determined look in the American's eyes.

"The game ends now, George," Edward said. "You are going to stop pretending and tell this woman that you know who she is and where she can locate her daughter."

George turned to look at Jean, standing near the door with Monica. "My wife is a state official," he told Jean with a pleading edge to his voice. "She doesn't know anything about my past. I never told her about Tiananmen."

"Mr. Wu," Monica said, her Irish lilt comforting and compassionate. "We don't want to do anything to endanger you or your family. But please—please—don't tell us again that you don't know who Jean is. We understand that you arranged for her to see her husband. And that took great courage. You've already taken a great risk to help her. Now help us get to the truth."

But George was already shaking his head with resentment and resignation. "Do you actually believe the truth will make any difference?" he spat.

"The truth is the difference," insisted Monica.

"No," George answered angrily. "The truth only makes reality harder to live with. A lot harder.

The truth is that Gus and Jean were my friends. But the reality is that it is still dangerous to acknowledge that. The truth is that democracy is a wonderful dream. Reality is that most Chinese don't want that dream as much as they want simple stability. The truth is that China is not what it could be. The reality is that it is not what it used to be. The truth can get you killed. Reality keeps you alive. So, I ask you. What do you want from me? Truth? Or reality?"

"I want my daughter!" Jean exclaimed. Her voice sounded powerful and potent in the stillness of the office. Jean stepped up to George, looking him straight in the eye with an unwavering intensity. "I don't want to put you in any danger," she continued. "I want only one thing now. Where is she, George?"

The young man looked back at his old friend and, sensing the indomitable mother's love he was facing, felt his anger and bitterness seep away. They continued to lock eyes for another long moment before he spoke.

"I waited for you all night in the apartment," he said as he cast his mind back to the terror of those long-ago days. "All night I heard the shooting and the screams and the soldiers arresting people. I knew it was just a matter of time before they came for us, too. A neighbor came by to tell me that Gus was dead and that you had been arrested. So, I went into hiding and took the baby with me." He stopped, and it was obvious from the pain that crossed over his face that he was having difficulty continuing.

"Go on," said Jean gently, encouraging her old friend to continue, "What happened?"

"We made it deep into the south," George resumed. "I found a family who would take care of your daughter until I could come back for her. They were kind people, Jean. Good people. I knew she would be safe. The last time I saw her, she was drawing the symbol of Liberty Moon you'd taught her with a stick in the dust of the farmyard. She would do that all the time . . . as if it reminded her of you."

"The family," Edward asked. "Where are they now?"

George hesitated again, but there was nothing left to do now but tell the end of his story. "There are sometimes in the south country . . . ," he said in a low voice, ". . . terrible floods."

Jean stifled a cry and buried her face in her hands as Monica wrapped her arms around her, trying somehow to absorb the pain. "I'm so sorry," she said, the words turning to ashes in her mouth.

"Thousands of people died that year," George continued, relentless now, as he pushed on to his tragic conclusion. "I tried to find the family, but they were gone. There is a chance, of course, that she survived. There is always a chance. But I am afraid that I cannot tell you where she might be."

He turned to Edward, raising his voice against Jean's soft sobbing. "I named my company Liberty Moon," he explained, "in the hope that one day Piao Yue might grow up and recognize it and make the connection. It was a slim chance, but our hopes have hung on such slim chances many times before. Just as I never imagined that it would be Jean who would find me this way." He tried bravely to smile, to bring some flicker of hope to this hopeless situation.

"How long have you known about Gus?"

Monica asked, trying to tie up the loose ends in her own mind.

"About a year," replied George, turning now to face the angel. "A state official, a man who works with my wife, mentioned at dinner one evening that he had heard of a poet, a political prisoner, who had miraculously survived a bullet in the back while he was in Tiananmen. It took a while to track him down—"

"Without jeopardizing yourself, of course," Edward said caustically.

"Of course," was George's equally cold reply. He looked back to Jean. "I hope seeing him gave you some peace," he said to her tenderly.

Jean nodded, a resolve growing behind her own eyes, an expression of some newfound strength and purpose. "It gave me more than that, George," she told him. "When I saw his face, I remembered who I was . . . and who I still am. I realized that I was no longer afraid. Tell me, George, what will you have to see before you, too, are no longer afraid?"

Without waiting for an answer, she turned and walked out of the office, leaving the others behind.

Edward watched her go and, torn between following her and letting her go, he turned to George.

"Is she in danger?" he asked.

"She is in this country illegally," George answered with a shrug. "She is a dissident who has gone unpunished. She has been recognized, and I'm sure they want to find her before she can make any more trouble."

"What kind of trouble?" Monica asked with a sudden foreboding.

George looked over to her as if the answer to her question must be obvious to all. "She spoke to her husband before he died," he said. "She now knows the truth and the reality."

Chapter Fifteen

*J*ean plunged back onto the crowded street outside George's office, the sidewalk even more difficult to navigate as commuters rushed for the evening buses and subways and taxis and bicycles that were already clogging the city. Her eyes were nearly blinded by her tears, but there was a new determination in her step, as if she had suddenly discovered the path that would bring her back to the beginning, to a place where she could start to make things right again. Her passion to balance the scales of justice and speak truth was restored.

Jean was so set on walking that path with all

the new dignity and courage she felt coursing through her veins, that she hardly noticed the leaflets left by the soldiers fluttering at her feet. On each, the photo of her looked out to some distant horizon, where the potential for freedom and liberty seemed to be dawning like the sun of a new day. She stopped then, knelt and picked one up, speaking a silent promise to that young woman that had once been her. Freedom is a state of mind, she proclaimed to herself. True liberty comes when you are no longer afraid.

Across town, Edward and Monica returned to the hotel, where they immediately spotted Alex at the front desk, picking up the day's messages from the desk clerk.

"She may have left us a note," Monica said to Edward as they approached the reception area, and Alex turned at the familiar sound of her voice.

"Have you seen Jean?" was Edward's first question to his friend.

"Well," replied Alex laconically, "what with her being a fugitive and all, I didn't exactly expect her to come waltzing through here again."

"Please, Alex," Monica pleaded. "Was she here at all?"

Alex sighed, then leaned in close with confidential information. "I think I might have seen her walking out when I came down," he revealed.

"Excuse me, Mr. Tanner," said the desk clerk, his formerly arrogant attitude evaporating. He spoke in a low and urgent voice and, for the first time, Monica and the others realized they had a friend. "The lady who is not here?" he said. "She left this."

He handed over a folded slip of paper, which Edward opened to read out loud.

Edward,

Thank you for all you have done. Please thank Monica for me as well. It is possible that we will not see each other again. George was right. Reality is the safest route. But I have nothing left to lose now. And so, I have the luxury of living in the truth and for the truth. I'm going to make sure

the whole world knows the truth about my hus-
band. You are a kind man, Edward. I hope some-
day you will find truth in your own peace.

Jean.

He looked up at the others, his eyes full of
concern as he contemplated the implications of
Jean's words.

"Where was the last place she lived in truth?"
Monica asked, pondering the riddle at the heart
of Jean's message. It took Edward only the blink
of an eye to answer the question and another
blink for him to convey it to Monica with a worried look. Together they turned and hurried out
the hotel's revolving doors.

Even at that late hour, Tiananmen Square was
bustling with tourists snapping pictures and trades-
men hawking their wares. The huge expanse, as
large as several football fields laid end to end,
was swept periodically by flocks of pigeons, dis-

turbed in their hunt for food by children playing happily between the legs of the grown-ups.
To one side, the imposing edifice of the Forbidden
Palace caught the fading light of the sun and the
row of Chinese flags outside fluttered in a mild
breeze that also kept aloft a dozen kites, stark
against the azure sky.

At one side of the square, a group of American
tourists, identifiable by their expensive traveling
togs and high-end cameras, was being shepherded
by a guide who pointed out the sights as she
spoke through a megaphone. Not far off, a pair
of policemen kept watch, failing to notice the
young woman who was moving with deliberate
intent toward the gaggle of tourists.

"Behind me," the guide droned through the
booming funnel of the megaphone, "is one of the
government buildings of the People's Republic of
China. Now, if you look the other way, toward the
north, you will see the view most people associate
with Tiananmen Square, the Gate of Heavenly
Peace. Now we'll be heading into the Great Hall
of the People." The tour guide pointed toward the
huge structure near them. "Right this way, please."

As the group began moving out, two older ladies in shorts and tennis shoes approached the guide with a request to have their picture taken. She obliged, setting down the megaphone and, in that moment, Jean saw her opportunity. Rushing through the crowd, she grabbed it and moved resolutely up the stairs of the Great Hall. Turning, she faced the crowded square and from her pocket pulled the incriminating leaflet showing her picture, taken in this very square so long ago. Lifting the megaphone to her mouth she cleared her throat and began to speak, in strong, clear, and unhurried Chinese.

"Citizens of the People's Republic of China!" she cried as her voice boomed out across the expanse. "My name is Zhang Jiang Li. I am the woman in the photograph the police are searching for."

Already bystanders, foreign and Chinese, had begun to gather around her. The police, too, had taken notice and were pushing their way toward her through the crowd.

"My husband was a poet," Jean continued, paying no attention to the approaching authorities. "He yearned for the freedom to speak his mind. To practice his faith. To write from his heart. He wanted nothing more than to expose the cruelty of this government, to share with all of you the dream of democracy."

From a short distance away, a group of young teenage girls, a few of them holding on to the strings of airborne kites, were crossing toward the steps where Jean spoke. The crowd, getting thicker by the moment, impeded the police, who shouted for her to cease and desist, their voices lost in the loud echo of the megaphone.

"Do not believe the official reports!" Jean was shouting now. "Do not believe the official reports! My husband did not renounce his participation in the student movement here in Tiananmen Square in 1989. His last words were words of love for his country! Do not believe the official—"

The words died on her lips as she noticed, floating in the twilight sky above her, in the flotilla of children's kites, one kite in particular. Beautiful in its simplicity, soaring high above the others, its paper painted not with the traditional Chinese symbols of birds and butterflies but with an elegant cipher that caused her to sharply catch her breath. There, hung in the sky above all earthly care, was a half-moon with a flame at its crescent—the Liberty Moon.

Hardly daring now to breathe, Jean traced the kite string with her eyes to the crowd of young girls gathered near the steps. The thin line of the string terminated in the small and delicate hands of a thirteen-year-old, her hair in pigtails, her eyes turned to the hovering kite. At that precise moment, the girl turned to face Jean, as if she felt her mother's eyes resting on her.

"Piao Yue!" cried Jean, her voice piercing the air despite the fact that she had dropped the megaphone. "Liberty Moon! Piao Yue! It is me . . . your mother!"

The police, bounding up the steps of the Great Hall, finally reached her and, one on each side, began to forcefully pull her away, back down into the square. At that moment Monica and Edward emerged from the back of the crowd, fighting their way toward their captive friend.

"Jean!" cried Monica as they finally pushed through to the base of the steps, but the angel's cry went unheeded. Instead, Jean was staring into the crowd searching for her daughter, even as the police half dragged her away.

Desperately, Monica turned and peered upward, trying to see what had captured Jean's attention, and fixed immediately on the Liberty Moon kite, bobbing and weaving in the darkening sky. Torn now between trying to help her friend and tracing the kite string to its source, Monica was nearly toppled by the crush of people, all straining to catch a glimpse of the unauthorized excitement in front of the Great Hall. Above the milling crowd she heard Jean's voice calling helplessly to her daughter, "Piao Yue! No! No!" Police whistles sounded shrilly as the officers began dispersing the crowd, pushing Edward and Monica even farther away from Jean.

"Edward! Look!" shouted Monica, pointing into the sky. But it was too late. The Liberty Moon kite had disappeared, and they were just able to catch the quickest glance of a group of schoolchildren being herded away by their teacher. The crowd surged again and they were shoved back to the perimeter of the teeming square.

Chapter Sixteen

Darkness fell over Tiananmen Square with austere finality as the tourists and peddlers slowly dispersed, leaving Monica and Edward alone on the steps of the Great Hall of the People, silent and stunned by the events they had witnessed not a half hour before. A numbing sensation that seemed to radiate from their hearts, dulling each part of their body and spirit until they felt dead inside.

"So what can we do?" asked Edward despondently. "Call the American Embassy?"

Monica shook her head. "She's not an American citizen," she reminded him.

"A lot of good that's done her," was Edward's bitter rejoinder. "Not once in my life have I ever had the urge to stand in the middle of Times Square and speak my mind about anything. But, all of a sudden, it's nice to know I can."

Monica was only half listening, turning over their dwindling options in her mind. "Okay," she calculated, "so the embassy is out. Going to the police will obviously get us nowhere . . ."

"I'd give every dime I have to get her out," Edward said with a sudden and fierce conviction.

"I don't think money is the answer," Monica replied, then added with a firm voice of unshakable faith, "but love can move mountains."

Edward shook his head sadly. "I'm not exactly the love type," he said. Then, realizing how inadequate mere words were to express how he felt, he tried again. "She's very . . . special, isn't she?"

"Yes," Monica agreed. "Yes, she is."

Once the admission had been made, Edward felt the emotions, so long denied and delayed, begin to rush up and over him. Suddenly, he wanted to tell the whole world about his feelings toward this one precious woman, but, for the moment, had to content himself with the ear of a willing angel.

"I mean," he said, turning to face Monica, "I know what being in love feels like but this is . . . deeper."

"In what way?" Monica asked, if only to allow Edward the chance to keep opening up.

"Well," replied Edward, once again struggling to find words to match what was welling up in his heart, "when we were there, in that factory, and I realized that her husband was still alive, I felt something I'd never felt before. It wasn't jealousy . . . far from it. It was happiness. I was sincerely happy for her and for him . . . for them both."

Monica smiled, putting her hand on his arm. "I'm glad for you, Edward," she said. "Love like that nourishes the soul."

"You mean," he asked wryly, "the one I lost?"

"I mean, the one you're finding again."

They sat back, turning again to watch the last stragglers move across the enormous expanse of the square, their thoughts once again returning to Jean.

It would have been a shock for them to realize how close by their friend really was, not any farther than the far side of the square in a holding cell in a police station off a Tiananmen side street. Yet, while Jean may have been in close proximity, she was already worlds away from the life she had once lived and the freedom she had once cherished. Stripped of her papers and clothes and every other vestige of her Western identity, she had become nothing more than a number in the vast Chinese prison bureaucracy, a faceless addition to a roster of forgotten and nameless captives, dressed in drab prison garb and tucked away in a corner of a vast and uncaring environment.

Monica and Edward walked not five hundred yards from where Jean was incarcerated on their way back to the hotel, but it might as well have been five thousand miles. They were separated now by a gulf as deep and wide as any that ever spanned between human beings—the chasm of tyranny.

Edward, exhausted and demoralized, made his way alone back to his empty room where he sat on the edge of the bed with his head in his hands. After a moment, he pulled the leaflet photo of Jean from his pocket and stared at it as the silent minutes moved past. Meanwhile, unbeknownst to him, his solitude had come to an end with the invisible and angelic arrival of Monica and Tess. They stood on each side of this single, suffering mortal, seeing, from their spiritual vantage point, through to Edward's aching heart.

"He loves her, Tess," Monica said.

"That's good," replied Tess. "Because it's going to take a lot of love to go the distance now."

"And how far is that?" Monica wanted to know.

"As far as the Father sends us," was all the wise angel would say.

"Today, in the square," said Monica, suddenly recalling the vivid image in her mind, "I saw a kite . . ."

"Yes, I know."

"Is there anything we can do about it?" asked Monica, trying to keep the plaintive edge from her voice.

"Remember what I said?" Tess gently reminded her. "We're here to be the wind. We do our job right, and I promise you . . . that kite will fly again."

Their rustling voices passed over Edward, who continued to stare at Jean's picture as if, somehow, his longing could bring her back to him. It was that longing that took flight in the wind of the angels, wafting out over the vast and sleeping city down through the cavernous depths of the prison to the very cell where Jean lay asleep, curled on the floor. She opened her eyes, certain for a moment that someone had called her name, but heard only the approaching sound of footsteps.

A guard slipped a key into the clanking lock and swung the door open. Barking an order in Chinese, he grabbed her off the floor and pushed her out into the hallway, lit at a distance by a single dim and flickering bulb. He moved her along as she strained to hear her name whispered once again, as if in a dream.

Edward, too, dreamed that night, a fanciful flowing stream of images: Jean running through a high alpine meadow, trailing a kite behind her on a long silver string, while, in the distance, three shining beings watched in silent witness. He woke suddenly to the sound of a ringing phone and answered to hear the voice of Alex, summoning him back to the world of harsh reality.

A half hour later, Alex sat in Edward's room, sipping room service coffee while the young executive got dressed. Alex picked up the photo of Jean where Edward had left it on the nightstand and turned to his friend, wondering how best to broach a delicate subject.

"This may be the wrong time to mention this," he finally ventured. "But do you remember our game plan?"

"Which one?" replied Edward, cinching the knot of his tie. "The short-term or the long-term?"

"The one about turning the long-term into the short-term," Alex answered. "The very short-term." He stood up, crossed to his friend and stood behind him, his reflection visible in the vanity mirror where Edward was completing his morning routine. "You remember," Alex continued. "The one we agreed on back at the Purple

Pub in our senior year. We were going to play the game hard for twenty years, go to business school, buy and sell, divide and conquer, and then retire at age forty-two with more money than God and lots of time left to enjoy it. That game plan."

"I remember," said Edward, glancing at the reflection behind him in the mirror. "So?"

"So," Alex wanted to know, "are we still playing that game?"

Edward turned to face his friend. "I don't know," was all he could find to say.

Anger boiled up in the lawyer's voice. "You don't know?" he echoed. "Well, you better find out! Because you're risking everything for some woman you've only known for a few days."

"She's not 'some woman,'" responded Edward, trying to calm the flaring situation. "She is . . . a friend."

"And I'm not?" Alex demanded. "Please explain this to me, because for the past twenty years, I've been under the impression that we were friends. You and me . . . against the world."

Edward shrugged. "Maybe we were just a

couple of guys helping each other to make a lot of money."

"And you've got a problem with that?" asked Alex, genuinely puzzled.

A long moment passed as Edward thought out his reply. "Yes, I guess I do," he finally answered. "Now that somebody's helping me to become something better . . . something higher . . ."

"Spare me," was Alex's cutting reply. "I thought we were in business together, but apparently it's all become one big group therapy session. So why don't you just tell me what you want to do now. I mean, have you got a new game plan?"

"I think so," Edward said nodding. "I've decided I don't want to build a factory in China. I don't want to run the risk of seeing Jean being 'reeducated' while she's stamping 'Made in China' on our action-hero dolls." A lump rose in his throat. "I want to get out of this country, Alex. And I want to take her with me." He fixed his friend with an intense look. "That's what I am thinking."

It was the utter sincerity in his voice, the power of his conviction, and the certainty that resonated in his words that finally convinced Alex of what he had so long been unable, and unwilling, to admit—Edward Tanner was deeply in love. Whatever had come between them in the past few days, it was time now for Alex to come alongside, to do what he could and offer support in any way he knew how.

"Tell you what," Alex said, clapping Edward on the shoulder. "I'll go back to New York. Hold down the fort. You stay here. Do what you have to do."

Gratitude prompted Edward to grab his friend and give him a brief, but tight, bear hug. "Thanks," he said over Alex's shoulder. "I will."

Chapter Seventeen

Except for its size, the courtroom was a mirror image of Jean's cell—a windowless, harshly lit chamber with the barest utilitarian minimum of furniture and nothing in the way of decoration or decorum to suggest that this was a place where truth and judgment were determined and dispensed. There was no statue of blind Liberty holding out her scales, no philosophical motto from great jurists of antiquity, no robes of office or seal of state. Instead, at a long table at one end of the room sat four judges in military uniform, presided over by a chairman. Before them was a straight-backed chair into which two guards placed the accused—a handcuffed Jean, still dressed in her soiled prison garb, her hair uncombed and her face smudged with dirt.

As the chairman fixed her with a stern and admonitory look, a bailiff brought forward the case file. A brief glance among the judges determined the nature and gravity of the crimes, and the chairman signaled for the advocate, a mousy man in an ill-fitting suit standing beside Jean, to step up.

"Are you the advocate for this case?" the chairman asked in a clipped and imperious tone.

The lawyer cleared his throat nervously. "I am, Your Honor," he squeaked.

Jean shot a look at him. "I don't know you," she said, then turned to the panel of judges. "Your Honors," she said, "please . . . I don't know this—"

"Silence!" commanded the chairman, slamming his fist on the table. "The trial will commence."

Jean sank back in her chair. What was the use of speaking out, of trying to defend herself or speak up for her beliefs? The outcome of her trial had been determined from the outset. Everything else was just a formality.

From the back of the room, a silent, invisible presence witnessed the proceedings with the same growing sense of foreboding, her angel's eyes watching this age-old ritual unfolding with a sadness too heavy to bear. Monica turned away as she saw Jean shrink before the might and power of the state, turned away from the tawdry tableau of the strong once again crushing the weak.

Across town, a desperate Edward was pouring out his frustration and rage against a country and a system that could allow such injustice, venting his anger at the only person left who might be able to tell him why the life of the woman he loved was hanging so precariously in the balance.

"Remember her?" he said between clenched teeth as he slammed down the leaflet photograph of the young Jean on George's desk. George looked up at him, his face the implacable mask of a man who had learned to survive by hiding his deepest emotions. "She told me you were her friend," Edward continued. "Now is the time to prove it."

"How?" George asked, as if the request were only the delirious demand of an uncomprehending foreigner.

"Help her," Edward answered, even angrier when he heard the skepticism in George's voice. "Find her a good lawyer. Get her out on bail."

George laughed, a single bitter bark from the back of his throat. "I can't even begin to educate you on the ignorance of that statement," he told Edward with something near contempt curdling his words.

Edward leaned over the desk, torn between punching out or pleading with the man in front of him. "Look," he said, deciding on the latter course. "Just tell me what it will take to get her out of there." He stopped, searching for and finding a spark of human compassion in George's eyes. "Please," he added, hoping to fan the spark into a flame.

George opened his mouth to speak again, then hesitated and dropped his eyes to the crumpled picture of Jean that lay before him. He sighed, then looked up again at Edward. Maybe there was no use in trying to tell this man what it was like to live in China, to yearn for freedom and to have that yearning denied year after year until hope itself was extinguished like a flame in a cold wind. Maybe it was useless . . . but he owed it to Jean, to Gus, to himself to try.

"Listen," he said, as outside the window the routine rhythms of big-city life droned on, "I want you to try to understand what I'm about to tell you. Most everyone who was arrested for participating in the Tiananmen Square demonstrations was given a three-year sentence. Some, like Gus, were rearrested even before they returned to their homes. Those who weren't soon discovered that they couldn't get jobs anymore, and that no matter where they went, there was always someone following behind. The ones who could get out, who could escape to the West, didn't come back. Jean was the exception and, because she dared to return, she is a thorn in their side, daring them to do something about her impudence and defiance. She is forcing them to deal with her, almost as if she were tying her-self to the stake and lighting the match for them. Tell me, Mr. Tanner, did she ever reveal to you why her nickname was Jean?"

"No," Edward whispered, fearing now what the reason might be. The stake. The flames. Suddenly, it was all falling into place.

"It's French for Joan," was George's response. "Of Arc. She knows exactly what she's doing. She can be more trouble to the authorities behind bars than she ever was outside prison. She knows that if she stays in jail, she'll become a martyr, a cause célèbre. She has made the choice to turn herself into a bargaining chip for some UN resolution or U.S. trade agreement. She's a huge risk for the government. One they simply can't afford."

Edward nodded, acknowledging the hard truth behind the political realities George was illumi-nating. "They can't leave her out," he said, "and they can't keep her in."

"Exactly," said George. "And the sooner her situation becomes international news, the safer she will be. Once the world knows she exists, they will have no choice but to keep her alive."

"Alive?" Edward repeated, a cold chill racing down his spine. "What are you saying?"

"Just this," replied George. "It's all going to happen very fast . . . if it hasn't happened already."

In the austere courtroom, it was as if George's grim prediction were being played out in pantomime, and as he spoke he described with chilling accuracy the fate that Jean was, even then, facing. As she sat slumped in the straight-backed chair, she watched with numb despair as the judge closed her case file and nodded to the guards. As her ineffectual advocate snapped shut his briefcase and walked out a small side door, she was lifted to her feet and led out under the stern and unrelenting gaze of the judges.

It was this same scene that, back in the office, George was describing to Edward in excruciating detail. "She'll go on trial," he was saying. "It may last only a matter of minutes. She'll be found guilty and returned to her cell. There she will remain, maybe for years, sitting in the dark until she grows weak and sick."

The sound of the slamming cell door echoed down the prison hallway as Jean was thrust back into the tiny, cramped enclosure and sank to the floor, now officially a nonperson, in a nonplace, without a history, without a future.

It was an echo of finality that Edward could almost hear as he listened, with growing horror, to George's unsparing account. "When she gets a fever or her teeth become infected," he said, "she won't get medical treatment. Or, if she manages to survive the terrible conditions, she might 'slip on the floor' during an interrogation and die of a cerebral hemorrhage or a broken back . . ."

"No!" shouted Edward, grabbing George by the collar. "That can't happen! I won't let it!"

"You can't stop it," George relentlessly continued. "But perhaps you are right. Perhaps it will happen this way: Some common criminals will suddenly have the urge to beat her to death in exchange for a shorter sentence."

"Stop it!" screamed Edward, still hanging on to George's shirt and now shaking him violently.

"Why are you so angry with her? It's almost like you want it to happen!"

George jerked back, freeing himself from Edward's grip. "I thought you Americans considered us Chinese 'inscrutable,'" he said. "Yet you can't read what is in my heart."

"But why?" was all Edward could say.

"Because she doesn't understand how it works," responded George, then checked himself. "No, wait. That's not right. She does understand how it works. It's just that she refuses to accept it. And it is that refusal that bothers me so much."

The flicker of a pained smile crossed Edward's lips. "And that is exactly what I love about her so much . . ."

On the desk the phone rang, startling both men like a sudden alarm, portending disaster. George picked up the receiver, listened silently, and hung up again. "The trial is over," he said quietly.

"What happened?"

"She was given a ten-year sentence," replied George, and the two men stared at each other as the full horror of the moment began to sink in.

Chapter Eighteen

*W*ell, I must say, it's a very unusual request." Tess pursed her lips as she walked with Monica and Andrew through the same serene park that had previously served as their Beijing rendezvous. The three angels were deep in conversation, discussing the heavenly protocol of Monica's earnest entreaty.

"But," Monica responded, "it's not as if it hasn't been done before."

Andrew put a hand on her shoulder. "It's quite an act of sacrifice, Monica."

"No," she replied with firm conviction. "It's not a sacrifice. It's a privilege." She turned to the senior angel. "Tess, when this all began, you told me it was about being given a chance to make a difference. Well, this is my chance. And I want to take it."

Tess shook her head, still doubtful. "We just don't know how long it could take," she speculated. "Maybe the whole ten years."

It was Andrew's turn to shake his head. "No," he said thoughtfully. "I don't think it will be that long."

Both Tess and Monica nodded. It was clear what Andrew was getting at.

"Well," allowed Tess, "in that case, it makes sense. At least to me. But, it's not up to me. It's up to the Father." She turned with a loving smile to Monica, "Ask Him, Baby," she urged. "He'll tell you what to do."

Monica nodded, hugging them both before taking a small route off the main path, already beginning to reach out and seek the divine guidance that was always just a prayer away.

"Lord," said Tess, offering up her own prayer as she watched the angel walk away. "Be with my little one." She took Andrew's hand and, together, they watched the wondrous Chinese moon as it began to peek over the rooftops of the city.

Hidden far from the light of that moon, Jean awoke suddenly in her damp cell, stirred by the sudden intuition that someone had entered the room. A strange, shimmering light shone in one corner of the tiny cell and, shielding her eyes from the unaccustomed brightness, she peered into it, making out the figure of a woman dressed in white. But it was not the flowing gown of some angelic garb, but rather a simple cut, a padded jacket and pants, made of a fabric as pure and as unsullied as anything Jean had ever beheld.

For a moment she started in fright. Then, lulled by an overwhelming sense of comfort and safety and the inborn conviction that she, after all, could only be dreaming, she turned on her side and went back to sleep, as Monica settled down in the corner to watch over her in the long, dark night.

When it broke, dawn brought with it the clattering of steel trays and the slamming of iron bars—the routine of prison life, not so different from any other morning ritual. Jean stirred, woke and, half remembering a wonderful dream she had had, sat up and rubbed the sleep from her eyes. When she opened them again, Monica stood before her.

"Monica?" Jean said, hardly trusting the evidence before her eyes.

"Hello, Jean," Monica replied, and her voice seemed to be emanating from a place inside Jean herself.

"What are you—how did you get in here?" she stammered.

Monica smiled. "Not the way you did," was her reply.

"I don't understand," said Jean, now not quite sure she was actually awake.

Monica stepped forward, the shimmering light moving with her. "It was a terribly brave thing you did in the square the other day, Jean," she began. "Standing up like that . . . defending your husband and proclaiming the truth."

Jean sighed. "I thought I had nothing left to lose." She shook her head, as if trying to dislodge the final irony that lingered there. "But, Monica," she continued, "my little girl. I saw her . . . I looked right into her face. She is . . . alive."

If great joy and inexpressible sorrow could coexist in a single space, it was in the space of Jean's words.

"I know," Monica replied. "I know."

"One minute more," Jean said, fresh tears welling where she thought no tears could ever fall again, "and I would have seen her before I stood on the steps and began to speak. And I could be holding her right now . . ." She sobbed, a wrenching sound that had no place to escape in the tiny cell. "Right now . . . in my arms."

"Jean," Monica said, and her voice full of compassion and understanding of a whole other realm of existence. "You couldn't have known. You did only what you knew you had to do. And, because of that, a wonderful miracle occurred—God granted you the grace to see the face of Liberty Moon before you were taken away."

"There is no God in China," said Jean, bitterness and disbelief taking the place of her tender tears.

"Oh, yes, Jean," Monica replied as the light around her seemed to grow suddenly brighter. "Yes, there is. And He loves you. I know because it is He who sent me here to be with you . . . to encourage you. You see, Jean, I am an angel."

Jean blinked, then swallowed hard. Whatever part of her rational mind had discounted Monica's words was quickly and completely overwhelmed by the stirring in her spirit confirming that, yes, this was true—an angel was standing before her, an actual angel. "I'm not afraid of you," she said, as if she were surprised by her own acceptance.

"Good." Monica smiled. "You're not supposed to be."

"When I was a little girl in the orphanage," Jean remembered, "I used to think that I had an angel watching over me."

"You did," Monica assured her. "And you do now. You could say I volunteered for the job.

You see, I admire you so much, Jean . . . your courage and your passion. I believe that I have as much to learn from you as you have to learn from me."

"And . . . what must I learn?" Jean asked haltingly after a moment.

Monica moved closer and the light around her now bathed Jean. "That there is no one left to trust now," she said. "No one but the One who created you. The One who loves you . . . so much."

"Am I going . . . to die?" Jean asked in a small voice.

"Yes," Monica answered simply.

"And will you stay here with me?"

"Of course," said Monica.

"Through everything?" Jean wanted to know.

Monica nodded, reaching out to stroke Jean's dark hair. "I want to help you die with as much courage and dignity as you lived."

"Then tell me," Jean said, with all the trust and confidence of a child, as she took Monica's hand and held it to her cheek. "Tell me about God."

For Edward, the day had begun with a dull ache in his heart that had bled over from the long night before. Wandering aimlessly though the streets of Beijing, blind now to the exotic sights and sounds that once assailed his senses, he found himself, as late morning moved slowly toward the lunch hour, back on the street of Jean's old apartment.

It was as if his feet, unbidden, had brought him back to this place and, once he realized where he was, he could only let them carry him farther, to the destination he now knew he had intended to reach all along.

Moving though the open door of the building, he passed down the dingy hallway and out into the courtyard, moving unerringly toward the small hiding place where Jean had secreted the few precious artifacts of her former life. Glancing around to make sure he was alone and unwatched, Edward moved the board away from the hole and, reaching in, pulled out one of the yellowed pamphlets that Jean and Gus had printed on their kitchen table press. He flipped through it, finding page after page of elegant Chinese calligraphy. Slipping it into his pocket, he hurried back down the hallway and out onto the street where he hailed a passing cab and headed back to the hotel.

In the backseat of the cab, he pulled out the pamphlet again and turned the pages, more slowly this time, lingering over the strange but beautiful symbols, each with a different and subtle shade of meaning, each drawn by the hand of Jean Chang, the woman he loved. He already knew what his next move was going to be. It might be difficult . . . virtually impossible, in fact, but with the help of a Chinese-English dictionary and a little perseverance, he was determined to translate the pamphlet to discover what she had written there.

Chapter Nineteen

$\mathcal{L}$unch in the prison was a bowl of lumpy porridge and a glass of brown, tainted water, but, since it was the first meal she had eaten in more than a day, Jean wolfed it down like a gourmet Chinese feast. Between bites, seated cross-legged on the floor across from Monica, she carried on an earnest conversation, part confessional, part interview, part eulogy, with the angel.

"I hope," Jean said, her large, liquid eyes reflecting her sincerity, "that what I have done can help to change even one person's life. Then I know I will have made a difference."

"You've already made a difference," was

Monica's soft reply. "A difference in Edward. He cares for you very much, you know."

"I care for him, too," Jean admitted, then sighing, added, "I would have liked to have told him that. I would have liked that very much."

From outside the cell, the thunder of pounding boots was heard approaching. The young woman and the angel hardly had time to exchange a look before the door slammed open and the cramped space was filled with soldiers. Hoisting Jean off the floor, they half dragged and half shoved her into the hall and down a clanging flight of metal stairs bolted to the concrete walls.

"Monica?" she cried out as the guards shoved her along a row of identically barred doors.

"I'm here, Jean," Monica replied, although she remained invisible to everyone else.

"I'm scared," Jean admitted. "Please, tell me something about God."

Monica's voice seemed to drift along down the hallway, following Jean like a whisper, heard softly in her ear. "When you pass through the rivers, I will be with you," Monica recited. "When you walk through the waters, they will not overtake you. When you walk through the fire, you will not be burned . . ."

An interrogation room waited for Jean, yet another in an endless labyrinth of anonymous, airless, and dimly lit chambers that honeycombed the government palace. Falling to the floor beside a table and chair, Jean watched as the guards turned on their heels and exited, purposely leaving the door open behind them. A moment later, Monica appeared. "What's going on?" she asked.

Jean looked up to where the angel stood, visible now. "Monica," she said. "Listen to me very carefully. She had a kite, decorated with a moon and a flame. She knows who she is. I believe that. I must believe that."

The light around Monica began to flicker like a guttering candle. "Jean," the angel repeated, her voice rising in alarm. "What's going on?"

"Listen!" Jean insisted. "Tell her how much I love her! And promise me you will tell her the truth. She is the daughter of a poet. She deserves to hear the truth. She will know what to do with it. Say it, Monica. Say it!"

"I promise," Monica repeated slowly, "I will

tell her the truth . . . and she will know what to do . . ."

She stopped as, in the doorway, several large and brutish female prisoners appeared, their long shadows cast over Jean where she lay, crouched on the floor. As they moved into the room, she instinctively backed away, but with no place left to go, she turned to face her tormentors . . . her executioners. At that moment, the angel beside her realized what was about to happen. "No!" shouted Monica as loudly as she could. But Jean was the only one who could hear her cry and, for Jean, there was nothing that could stop what was about to happen.

As the thuggish inmates began kicking and punching the cowering prisoner on the floor, Monica threw herself over Jean's body, covering her as a mother would her only child. The blows continued to rain down, sharpened now by brutal curses and taunts, but what the attackers could not see was that their assault was being absorbed by the spiritual creature that lay across Jean's supine body. Screaming more in terror than in pain, Jean held tightly to Monica as the prisoners redoubled their efforts, dragging her to her feet and throwing her against the wall like a sack of stones, only to see her stand dazed and unhurt under their most vicious attack. Sometimes it appeared as if the mortal human was recoiling from their blows, and at other times, as if a creature dressed in white and surrounded by light stood in for her.

Slowly the prisoners ceased their bloody work, the fierce light of violence fading from their eyes to be replaced by one of puzzlement and the first inklings of fear.

From outside, where they had been smoking cigarettes and listening to the mayhem, the guards burst in, angered to see Jean still standing unbowed, while the prisoners stood back, mouths agape. Jean stared at them all, almost as surprised as they were to find herself uninjured and in no pain.

"You were ordered to kill her!" one of the guards shouted at the prisoners. "Do your duty!"

The most vicious of the women, her face scarred by a lifetime of abuse, shook her head as she stood stolidly, refusing to move. "She should be dead by now," she said with a snarl. "She is protected by a spirit. We cannot fight against a spirit."

Backing away from Jean, the prisoners crowded out the door, leaving the frustrated guards to finish the job. Grabbing their victim, they pulled Jean out of the room, dragging her back down the hall toward the metal stairway. "Monica!" Jean cried loudly, sensing for the first time the absence of her guardian angel.

But Monica could not rise. Battered and dazed, she lay in the corner of the cell until a hand reached down to help her to her feet. Looking up, she made out the face of Andrew and, taking his hand, pulled herself up and staggered out the door. She rushed down the hallway, past the rows of doors and the shouting prisoners locked behind them, until she came to the entryway leading into the stairwell. She looked up.

There, at the top of the well, Jean stood surrounded by the guards. There was only a moment for her to trade a look with the angel, a look that signaled they both knew what was about to happen.

Yet even in the inevitability of the moment, Jean and Monica both silently acknowledged God's mercy. Death, when it came, would not be a slow and painful ordeal at the hands of prisoners. He would take her quickly, with a minimum of suffering.

"I'm here, Jean!" cried Monica as above her, Jean closed her eyes and yielded herself over, in love and trust, to the care of her Creator. The guards shoved her backward down the steep stairs, and as she plummeted she called out once again for the angel that had stood by her side.

"Monica!" she cried, her voice broken now as her body hit the unforgiving steel rungs of the staircase.

"I'm here, Jean!" answered Monica as she watched the frail human body tumble broken and battered toward her. Then, as quickly as it had begun, it was over, and Jean lay motionless at the angel's feet. Monica knelt down and tenderly lifted her head, as she cradled Jean in her arms.

From above, all the guards could see was the lifeless body of their victim. Wordlessly they turned and tramped off, leaving Monica and Jean alone.

"Pro . . . mise . . . ," Jean whispered in a weakening voice.

"I promise," Monica said, her tears wetting the face of the woman in her arms.

Jean managed a weak smile. "Good," she said before a racking cough clutched at her chest. "Now," she said, barely above a whisper. "Tell me more . . . about God."

Monica's voice was weak, too, as she struggled to find the strength to grant her friend's last wish. "On this side, there is life," she reassured her. "And there, with Him, is life, also. And it is there that you shall behold Him . . . face to face . . ."

In the stairwell, a third figure now appeared, bathed in the same light as his fellow angel. Andrew knelt down next to Jean and Monica and, looking into the face of the young woman, asked in the kindest and most peaceful voice she had ever heard, "Are you ready to leave now, Jean?"

The answer could come only in an almost imperceptible nod before Jean's dark eyes seemed to stare at nothing and her body went limp in Monica's arms. "Good-bye," said the angel as she kissed the forehead of the empty vessel that had once been Jean Chang.

Chapter Twenty

$\mathcal{S}$lumped over the desk in his hotel room, his head bowed beneath a pool of light from a halogen lamp, Edward had passed into a deep and dreamless sleep. In his hand was the tattered pamphlet he had rescued from Jean's old apartment, while, to one side, an English-Chinese dictionary lay open.

Stirring slightly to relieve the stiffness in his neck, his arm swept the pamphlet to the ground where a hand reached down to pick it up and place it carefully back on the desk. The pure white prison clothes that Monica still wore glowed in the half light of the hotel suite.

"Edward," she said softly. "It's time to wake up." He stirred, roused from sleep by her gentle bidding. "Edward," she said again, and suddenly he was wide awake, remembering in a sickening rush everything that had happened over the course of the last terrible twenty-four hours.

"Where have you been?" he asked Monica, his voice still thick with the dregs of sleep. "What are you doing?" He looked around. "Wait a minute . . . how did you get in here?"

Monica reached out to lay a comforting hand on his shoulder. "Edward," she said, "I have something to tell you. Jean . . . she fell down a flight of stairs in prison. She's dead."

Edward staggered backward as if he had been slapped in the face. His mind reeled, and the world around him seemed suddenly to tilt out of control. He stared at Monica for what seemed an eternity before turning away in utter despair and putting his head in his hands. "Fell down a flight of stairs," he repeated, George's dire predictions echoing in his mind.

"She was . . . allowed to fall," Monica continued. "It was very fast. She felt no pain."

Edward shot a look at her, one full of anger and resentment. "Oh, yeah?" he said sarcastically. "And how would you know?"

"Because," answered Monica evenly, "I was with her."

As she spoke, the light around her body began to intensify, from a warm glow to a burning radiance so bright Edward had to shield his eyes. Certain now that the world he once knew so well, the world he had been determined to conquer, had become a place of nightmares and terror, he shrank back from her, his eyes reflecting the fear of madness that had suddenly infected him.

"Don't be afraid, Edward," Monica said. "You see, I'm an angel."

"I'm going insane," Edward stammered desperately. "Or I'm dreaming. Yes . . . that's it. I'm dreaming. None of this is true. Jean is still alive, and all I have to do is wake up and I'll—"

"No, Edward," Monica said, "it's all true. Jean is dead. And I am an angel. God sent me to be with you on this long and very difficult journey." She took his hand and, holding it in her own, knelt down in front of him. "Jean's journey is over," she explained, "and now she is at peace. But before she went we spent hours, just talking together about God and His love for her. And for you, too, Edward. You must believe that God loves you very much. And the 'coincidences' that seemed to bring you and Jean together, all became blessings in His hands. Crises became opportunities that you and Jean had the chance to embrace. And you took that chance. Both of you. Jean wanted you to know . . . she wanted me to tell you . . . that she cared for you very much. Because you had a chance to make a difference in her life. And you took it."

Edward began to sob. "I loved her," was all he could say.

"I know you did," Monica replied, squeezing his hand. "And I know that now your heart is broken. But God will mend it. You must simply trust Him with it now. Will you?"

"I miss her," was Edward's only answer.

"So do I," agreed Monica. "But I believe that you will see her again, Edward. That we both will. And until that time, there is a little girl right here who needs you."

Edward looked at her, his vision stained with tears. "What can I do?" he pleaded. "Please . . . tell me."

"Sleep now," was the angel's counsel. "In the morning things will look different. You'll be able to see more clearly."

Edward moved to the bed and fell back onto the pillow. His head felt too heavy for his neck, just as his heart felt too heavy to keep beating. Perhaps if he just closed his eyes for one brief moment . . .

When Edward opened them again, sunlight was pouring through the hotel windows. The traffic noise rose in a muffled symphony from the street below, and through the wall, in the room next to him, he could hear the discordant sound of a Chinese pop music radio station. In an instant his head was clear, and in another instant he was out the front door, his plan and purpose clearer in his mind than anything had ever been before.

George sat at his desk, sorting through a tall pile of mail as an associate hovered nearby. "Get this faxed to New York immediately," George was saying as he handed his assistant a contract draft. It was at that moment that the rumpled and puffy-eyed Edward appeared at the door.

The alarmed assistant stood frozen, uncertain what to do, until George nodded and, with a word of Chinese, sent him scurrying into the outer office. He gestured for Edward to sit down. "I heard . . . this morning," he said as Edward crossed to the chair in front of the desk.

Wordlessly, Edward pulled Jean's pamphlet out of his pocket and laid it on the scarred, wooden desktop. "How long will it last?" he quoted from his own translation. "This childhood of Liberty Moon? What must I do to save China?"

George was overcome by an unexpected rush of tears. "Save China," he repeated sadly. "We couldn't even save Jean."

"Do you remember the last thing she said to you?" Edward asked him.

"Yes," George answered, choking on the word. "I do."

"She said, 'What will you have to see before you are no longer afraid?'" Edward repeated. "She said, 'What will you have to see?'"

"I don't know," was George's despairing reply.

"How about a little girl's face?"

George, startled, could only stare. "What?" he asked dumbly.

"She's alive, George," Edward said with an intensity that sent a jolt through the businessman. "She's somewhere in Beijing. Some kind of school or orphanage. Jean saw her on the square. Now, I have a lot of money. And you have a lot of official connections. I have a joint venture I'd like to propose to you."

Edward smiled broadly and, for the first time since he'd met him, George looked like a man who had just had his life sentence commuted.

Three days later, it seemed to both men that the life sentence had been reinstated for George and, this time, for Edward as well. A fruitless journey through the maze of the Chinese government bureaucracy had yielded nothing and, dejected and demoralized, they walked back from their latest meeting—and latest blind alley—with still nothing to show for their efforts.

"So," Edward said as they made their way along a winding side street not far from Tiananmen Square, "that's it? No chance?"

George shook his head in sadness and frustration. "I'm afraid so," he replied. "Even with the large bribe you have put forward, we can't possibly tour every orphanage in the province. I'm beginning to think that there's a very good chance that Piao Yue has already been adopted and is no longer part of the system, anyway."

"I don't think so," said Edward, his lips pursed as he returned again to a persistent feeling that had remained with him since the moment he had awakened with a clear purpose, some days ago. "God wouldn't bring me this far to find a little girl who didn't need to be found."

George gave him a startled look. "God," he echoed. "Suddenly God is involved?"

"He's been there from the beginning, George. We just didn't know it."

"From the beginning of what?" George asked, his skepticism growing apace with his curiosity. Westerners were strange and exotic people . . . always looking for cause and effect in a random universe.

Edward considered the question for a moment as the two stopped at a fast-food cart to buy their lunch, a quick bowl of hot and tasty noodles. "You know," he finally answered, "I was kind of an orphan myself. After my dad split, my mom married this real jerk and I ended up spending most of my time with my grandmother. After she died, I bounced around from foster home to foster home. I remember wondering whether there was anybody out there that I really belonged to. And, at those times, I would always hang on to something my grandma would tell me. 'Eddie,' she'd say. 'You'll always belong to God. He'll never let you go.' I guess that somewhere along the way, I forgot that. But, it seems, He never forgot me."

George nodded, his own thoughts turning deeper, reaching toward a core of loneliness that he, too, suddenly realized he had been carrying around inside for a very long time. "This God you speak of," he said, turning to a man he had over the past few days come to consider a friend. "You speak of Him almost as if He were someone you know personally."

"Maybe," Edward replied with a slight smile. "One day."

"I have trouble believing in someone I can't see," George confessed. "I need proof."

Edward clapped his hand on George's shoulder as they strolled along. "Come on, George," he countered. "What about the air? Or the wind? You can't see them, either, but are you telling me—" he stopped dead in his tracks. "Wait just a minute," he said, as inspiration lit his eyes.

"What is it, Edward?" George asked, wide-eyed himself now, as the toy executive plopped his briefcase down on a nearby windowsill, snapped open its latches, and pulled out a strange construction of wood, string, and purple tissue paper. "What is that?"

Edward ignored the question as he began to unfurl Tess's portable kite, holding it in his hand and already feeling its tug as a passing breeze tried to lift it into the air. He turned to George.

"I need some paint," was his simple, urgent request.

A half hour later, Edward stood in the midst of a field of patchy grass in a small park in the middle of a Beijing business district. Watched by a still-baffled George, he tugged at the string in his hands, prompting the kite to dip and weave and then climb higher into the pale blue city sky. Even from this distance, George could plainly see the logo painted on the kite's purple skin— a half-moon with a flame nestled in the crescent.

For the remainder of the day, the American's strange behavior continued to baffle George. After flying the kite in one part of the city for an hour or more, Edward would reel it in, jump into a cab and, consulting a Beijing map he kept in his briefcase, ask to be driven to another park, sometimes within blocks of the previous one, sometimes in a far corner of the city. There he would jump out, set the kite free and wait patiently until he was prompted by some unheard voice to move on. Occasionally, when encountering a group of children with their own kites, he would carefully inspect each one for the telltale emblem until, satisfied that the matching Liberty Moon was not among them, he'd leave.

Each time, George had to resist the temptation to drag his friend back to the hotel where he could get some rest. Somethimes, he even smiled to himself at the intensity of this American. Edward was so convinced he had found a way to reach out to Jean's dauther, lost in a swarming city, and the sight of this eccentric Westerner flying a kite in his expensive business suit was at once strange and comical. But George stifled his laugh. Stranger things had happened in the last few days.

Chapter Twenty-One

It was late afternoon by the time the two men found themselves back at a familiar location—the quiet confines of the Garden of Peaceful Memories. Edward, his energies beginning to flag after the long day, launched the kite once more before settling down on a park bench to rest. George could see that he was tired, but still determined, and what had formerly been concern and even bemusement now turned into admiration. He knew that Edward's behavior was borne of a deep conviction, a conviction George could not help but respect.

"I'll get us some tea," George offered, and

Edward nodded, his eyes still turned to the kite above them. As George disappeared around a corner of the park path, Edward settled back on the hard bench seat, his body weary, but his spirit still alive with the extraordinary possibility sparked by his newly found faith. Agencies, officials, files, and formalities . . . they had tried it their way. Now it was time to try it God's way.

The realization came to him suddenly that, in this small slice of greenery in the middle of the vast city, he was, perhaps for the first time since he had arrived in China, completely alone. It was a rare enough occurrence in a city teeming with so many millions upon millions, and Edward took the opportunity to savor his solitude, to commune with the sky and the earth and the feeling of perfect harmony that existed between them. The Creator of all things had created this moment as well, giving Edward the ability to see and appreciate the perfection of the natural world and the grace and love that kept the sun in the sky, his heart beating within him . . . and the kite, hanging below the clouds, suspended on a breath of wind.

A deep serenity began to steal over him as he watched the mesmerizing motion of the kite, responding to every variation of the wind like a fish in the midst of an ocean current. His eyes began to grow heavy, his arm too tired to support even the feather weight of the kite string and, just at the moment when he was about to pass from wakefulness to sleep, he suddenly sensed someone approaching down the path.

As he watched, a group of schoolgirls, all dressed identically in a plain and unadorned uniform, emerged around the bend. One of them immediately caught his attention, and he guessed she was about thirteen years old. She held something in her hand, but so riveted was Edward to the haunting familiarity of her face that he took no notice at first, but simply watched, entranced as she came closer, chattering happily with her friends.

As the girls spilled out into the park clearing, under the watchful supervision of their teacher, the one who had caught Edward's eye looked up into the sky. Seeing his kite flying there, she followed its string back to his hand and, with the bold innocence of childhood, crossed over to him and stood, silent and face-to-face, solemnly regarding this strange grown-up who had found the time to fly a kite.

"Hello," said Edward, trying to keep the trembling out of his voice.

"Do you speak English?" the girl asked in a sweet, lilting voice that demonstrated her own precocious command of the language.

"Yes," said Edward, simply and slowly, as he inwardly gave thanks to God for what was unfolding before him.

The girl pointed to the flash of purple floating in the sky. "Kite," she said.

She lifted her arm to show him what she was holding in her hand. "Kite," she repeated, pleased with the progress of her impromptu English lesson.

Edward stared at the kite, his eyes fixed on the symbol of a half-moon with a flame at its crescent. He couldn't tell whether his heart had stopped beating, whether he was still breathing, whether time was standing still, or whether he had suddenly been lifted off the earth into a realm where God's grace shone forth in the face of a young girl.

"My name is Edward," he said as he managed to find his voice again. "What is your name?"

"My name is Piao Yue," the girl replied, first bowing, then sticking out her hand as she had been taught was the Western way.

Edward took the hand, feeling how small and delicate it was in his. They shook as Edward asked, "Do you know what your name means in English?"

"Yes," the girl said with a wide and radiant smile. "My mother taught me. It means 'Statue of Liberty.'"

The words released something in Edward, a cry of his soul as it reached up to embrace the goodness of the Creator, who, from the very beginning, had foreseen this moment, had planned and purposed for it to unfold with exact and perfect timing. Tears sprang up in his eyes as he gave silent thanks and acknowledged, for the first time since he was a child no older than the one that stood before him, that God was faithful and true and trustworthy.

George came around the bend, carrying a paper tray with two cups of tea. He stopped when he saw the young girl standing next to Edward. She was looking up into the sky, where Edward had released the kite, watching as it flew free, high above the trees and rooftops, floating away to find its destiny, as it had been lovingly made to do.

Epilogue

"It has been a pleasure, Mr. Tanner," said the front desk clerk as Edward signed his bill.

"Thank you very much," replied Edward, his Chinese heavily accented, but perfectly serviceable.

The clerk nodded approvingly. "You have learned much since you have been with us."

You have no idea, Edward thought, but only smiled and, bowing slightly, answered, again in Chinese, "Yes, I have."

He turned to where George stood, holding Piao Yue's hand as the bellboy loaded their luggage into the back of a waiting taxi.

"All set to go," he told them.

"I thought you'd like to know," George said, as Piao Yue let go of his hand and grasped Edward's, "that my wife was able to pull some strings . . ."

"I always had complete confidence in both of you," Edward interjected with genuine affection.

It was George's turn to smile. "The adoption papers will be finalized six months earlier than expected," he continued. "She'll be out of the orphanage and home with us by June."

Edward turned to the young lady holding his hand. "So maybe this means summer camp in Maine, after all," he teased.

"You said every summer," Piao Yue insisted. "You promised."

"Yes, I did," Edward replied. "And a promise is a promise."

He began walking to his waiting taxi as George and Piao Yue fell in step beside him.

"You'd think a little girl with an opportunity to live in America all year round would have jumped at the chance," George said.

"I just told her the truth," replied Edward as

they emerged onto the busy street. "And she knew what to do with it." He bent down. "Good-bye, Miss Liberty," he said, giving Piao Yue a hug. "I'll be seeing you soon."

"Good-bye," she answered in English.

Edward took a step toward the open taxi door, then turned around. "I almost forgot," he said to the young lady, still dressed in the simple uniform of an orphan. "I want you to practice your English every day. Then, when you come to see me next summer, you can tell me what this means."

He handed over the dog-eared copy of Jean and Gus's poetry pamphlet. Piao Yue looked at it solemnly before turning to him with the large, dark eyes of her mother and nodding. "I will," she said. "I promise."

Edward turned suddenly to keep her from seeing the tears in his eyes and climbed into the taxi. As they moved out into the heavy morning traffic, he noticed another passenger sharing the backseat with him.

"Monica," he said. "Will I ever see you again?"

Monica shook her head. "I don't think so. But I thought you might like to keep this."

From behind her on the seat, she produced a familiar construction of wood, string, and purple paper, festooned with the symbol of a moon and a flame—the Liberty Moon. Folding it up, she handed the portable kite back to Edward.

"How did you—" he began.

"It was lost," Monica said. "Now it's found. God is very good at that."

"Yes," said Edward, staring at the fragile beauty of the toy in his hand. "Yes, He is."

Monica looked out the window as they passed by the Garden of Peaceful Memories, a familiar landmark to her by now. "This is my stop," she said as the taxi idled at a light and, like Edward, turned away to hide her tears and opened the door, moving across the sidewalk without looking back.

Tess and Andrew sat on a bench near the koi pond as Monica approached. What the angel had been able to hide from Edward was immediately evident to her two coworkers.

"You okay?" asked Andrew as she sat next to them and wiped the tears from her eyes.

"Come on, Angel-Girl," said Tess with a hug. "I think it's time we were heading home."

Twenty-four hours and thousands of miles later, Edward's thoughts also turned toward home as he could feel the huge jet begin its descent and, over the cabin intercom, a soft chime signaled an announcement by the stewardess. He slipped the crumpled picture of a beautiful, pigtailed Chinese woman standing in the midst of Tiananmen Square back into his coat pocket as the speaker above crackled to life.

"Ladies and gentlemen," it said, "the captain has turned off the No Smoking sign, indicating our final descent into Kennedy International Airport. Please return your seat backs and tray tables to their original upright positions."

Edward obeyed as the airplane began its slow circle toward its final destination. He glanced out the window. The Statue of Liberty gleamed in the sunlight of a new day. Above her radiant crown, a white dove flew high on an invisible current of wind.

It was good to be home.

BAKER & TAYLOR